Prison 917

Samantha Nicklaus

This is a work of fiction. Any resemblance to actual persons, living or dead, or actual events is purely coincidental.

Reviews can be left on Amazon.com and GoodReads.com

SamanthaNicklaus.com

Twitter.com/SamNicklaus

Facebook.com/AuthorSamNicklaus

Copyright © 2017 by Purple Sun Media, LLC

Cover by Jonas Mayes-Steger of Fantasy & Coffee Design

Logo by Ren Oliveira

All rights reserved. This book or any portion thereof may not be reproduced or used in any manner whatsoever without the express written permission of the author except for the use of brief quotations in a book review.

Thank you to everyone who took the time to read this book. It means the world to me.

Part One 1
Part Two 49
Part Three 81

Part One

Before I even opened my eyes, I knew something was horribly wrong. Like that feeling you get when you bolt up in the middle of the night, sweating, because of a nightmare you can't remember. Like that, but it also smelled like rotting eggs.

I knew I was on my back, and when I opened my eyes, there was a cloudless blue sky above me. Had the smell not made my eyes start to water, I probably wouldn't have thought there was anything wrong.

Something rustled, and I turned my head to look at it. There was a small girl sitting up, her arms holding her knees against her chest. She couldn't have been more than seven, gold hair, brown eyes, and a cut just under her hairline. She didn't say anything to me. Didn't even look at me.

"Hey."

It came from the other side of me. I rolled my head over and looked. Above me stood a tall girl—or she looked tall because I was on the ground. She knelt down next to me. "Hey, are you okay?" she asked. "You can move, right?"

I sat up, slowly. The tall girl's hands followed me, ready to catch me. Up close, I could see how messy she was. Her brown hair was frizzy and looked like it had been hacked off, not cut. Under her left eye was a small dark purple mark; a black eye on the mend. She smelled like sweat and dirt, which made sense, looking at her closely. She gave me a little smile, showing off fuzzy teeth.

"You okay?" she asked, looking me over. Her voice was as rough as she looked.

"Yeah," I croaked out, my mouth and throat dry.

"Yeah, that happens," she said, looking around. "Sorry." I didn't know exactly what she was sorry for, but she stood up, looking around the field. I looked with her, and realized there were more people laying in the field. A lot more people, maybe thirty. A chill ran up my spine.

"Stay here, okay?" she said. She walked away before I got a chance to ask what was going on. I watched her walk over to someone else and kneel down next to them too.

I sat there, because what else was there to do? There was nothing but grass around us, maybe three inches high, higher in some places. In the distance, I could see a fence. It looked about twenty feet tall, but I was bad at guessing that kind of thing. In the other direction, there were buildings, maybe a mile away; they looked like a bunch of outhouses. The girl next to me sat in silence as well, just looking around.

More and more people started to wake up. The tall girl couldn't get to all of them at the same time. Some of them, upon waking, started to yell. One boy started to cry. Everyone else seemed to know where we were or had some idea what was happening. I wanted to ask someone, but no one looked my way and they were at least a few feet from me. I didn't want to yell across to them, and the tall girl had told me to stay where I was. The little girl next to me watched, silently. I didn't want to ask her either.

I had no idea how long it took for everyone to wake up, but eventually everyone was milling around. Some people wandered off, even after the tall girl told them not to.

"Hey!" she called, and everyone looked in her direction. "If you leave, we won't take you in. No one will." The few people who were wandering away started to wander back over. "Yeah, I thought so." She paused. "Alright, well, welcome. I'm Delany. I'm in charge of you."

It was quiet. "This is Prison 917. There are no guards here," she explained, pointing back towards the buildings in the distance. "We are in charge of ourselves. We are divided into groups. You are in Red group."

As she spoke, I came to the conclusion that I was in a coma, and this was all some kind of dream. My stomach growled. Something about this reminded me of playing capture the flag in middle school. Maybe I was on some kind of elaborate prank show.

"If you weren't aware, you're a criminal. We all are. You are marked with a number. The fence over there—" she pointed ahead of her, behind us. "Is electric. Not the fun kind of electric. It will kill you. There is no way to turn it off, no way to climb it, no way to go under it. If you decide prison isn't for you, the fence is your other option." As she spoke, I looked down at my arm. A number, 982642, was tattooed on it in perfect lettering, about four inches down from my wrist. I had no idea when it was done, but it didn't hurt. The skin around it was red, and I ran my thumb over it.

"You're supposed to laugh when I make a joke." This sounded rehearsed, like she did this a lot. People chuckled, for her sake.

"We are completely on our own, so if you are hungry or thirsty—get used to it." I could barely see her through the crowd of people, but it looked like she was smiling. "We aren't big on gifts. Come on, I'll give you the tour."

She turned and started to walk off, and we followed her. Some people, I don't know if they knew each other already or just made fast friends, talked and joked as we walked. I had never been to summer camp before, but it felt like that. I don't think the word prison had registered with me yet. As we walked, I made my way to the front of the group. My dad had told me once to always make friends with the meanest kid on the playground. Right now, I was pretty sure that was Delany.

It hadn't seemed hot before, but walking changed that quickly. I could see girls pulling at their shirts, trying to create a breeze. A few of the boys took off their shirts and wrapped them around their heads. I don't know how far we walked, probably a mile, but the little town hardly seemed to get bigger.

Once we could get a good view of it, it was very lackluster. Though, I guess I was expecting too much of a prison. One of the people behind me let out a long whistle.

We walked up to an archway, that had the circular fence surrounding the place not been a mile away, would have been an entrance. It was made of two cinderblock pillars, with a metal piece connecting them. Something had been painted on it once, but the paint was long gone and the sun had faded the lettering away.

Past that, the prison opened up in front of us. I had never used the phrase "shanty-town" before, but there was no other way to describe this. There was one cinderblock building in the middle of it all that had blocks removed at random. There was one spot I could see, where a hole had black scorch marks around it. The doorframe in front no longer had doors. The inside was dark, but I could see light coming in from above like there were holes in the ceiling.

There were smaller buildings to the left and the right, clearly self-made. They were made of plywood, a few cinder blocks, large chunks of metal, and a few of them just had some kind of dirty cloth draped over the top or sides. Each one was different, some standing perfectly straight, some leaning against each other, some so slanted I was amazed they were standing at all. Most of them must have been around six feet tall, and maybe five or six feet long, barely big enough to sleep in.

People, not us, but the people who lived there, were hanging around, careful not to get too close. We could see their heads duck around walls or eyes through holes in the houses. Delany followed our gaze and looked at them. A few of them skirted back when she looked. Everyone was dressed like we were—mostly jeans and t-shirts, a few girls in dresses or boys in sweats, but it was pretty uniform. "Don't mind them, they're harmless for now," she said, waving a hand.

She put back on her loud voice. "This is the town hall. We get it for a week at a time, and each group takes turns. Lucky for you, it's our week."

"What do we do with it?" someone asked.

Delany shrugged. "It's the best shelter we have." I didn't think that was a real answer.

She turned and led us inside. It was a mix of what looked like old factory pieces, metal tables, and just scraps of metal. The place looked like a junkyard, everything stacked and pushed against each other. Delany moved through the heaps of junk like a deer through the woods; graceful and with little effort. We, on the other hand, struggled. We had to wiggle our way in between machines and metal sheets to follow her. There was a bit of a clearing in the center of the room, and we stopped there. "This is where we hold the group meetings. Most of them are private, but I need a new number two, so maybe one of you will find yourself here one day." Delany almost looked sad for a moment, before there was a loud crashing sound.

Some people cried out, shocked at the sound. I took a step closer to Delany, who hadn't seemed phased at all.

A tall, skinny boy with a mop of brown hair walked forward. He was wearing ripped jeans, no shoes, and no shirt. He had tied a scrap of some yellow cloth to hold back his hair, but it wasn't working too well. I counted his ribs as he moved towards us.

"Rabbit," Delany scolded, sounding more bored than annoyed. "Get lost."

He flashed a charming smile. "What, I can't say hi?" He was moving towards us the whole time, his hands raised as if to prove he was innocent.

"They're Red, get lost," Delany said, more threatening this time. It was like watching something on one of those animal shows, where you know two animals are about to fight. It made my chest hurt.

Rabbit didn't stop smiling as he walked towards us. Something about him made him seem like a threat, but I wasn't sure what it was. Maybe it was just how Delany looked at him.

I was on the edge of the group, next to Delany, and he started to walk towards me. I looked at Delany, but she just rolled her eyes. Rabbit held out his hand to me. "Hey, I'm Jack. People here call me Rabbit." I didn't move. "What, are you afraid of Delany? She's a sap, trust me." He took my hand and kissed it. "There's always room in Yellow if you get—"

Delany stepped so she was behind Rabbit, ripping him away by the back of his neck. He winced for a second, then flashed a smile. "Get lost before you lose some teeth," she said in a low growl. The hair on the back of my neck stood up. She pushed him away, and he took a few steps back, so he wasn't in her range anymore. Rabbit held both hands up in surrender.

"Just trying to welcome the newbies," he said, innocently. "Good luck with them, Red." He winked at her as he left.

"Don't pay attention to Rabbit," Delany said, to the group, but mostly to me. "Come on." She started to move again, back the way we had come. I was careful to follow in Delany's footsteps exactly, and still I couldn't manage to keep pace with her.

She waited for everyone to catch up. Once we were all out of the machinery jungle, she spoke again. "Like I said, there are groups here. We are Red, there's Yellow, which Rabbit weaseled his way into leading, Purple, Green, Blue, Orange, and Pink."

"Good thing we didn't get Pink," someone joked.

"Yeah, good thing, they had a bit of a cannibalistic streak in them," Delany said, stone-faced. "We sleep, eat, and are friends with our own." I didn't know if that was a rule or a suggestion, but I wasn't going to question it.

Delany started to walk again, leading us out of the building and to the left. It was clear we were in the Red group, there were patches of red flying or hanging from almost every little house there. There were maybe a hundred of them, it was hard to tell. They weren't laid out on any kind of system, just thrown wherever. People had worn paths between them, making little dirt roads.

"I've assigned you rooms for now," Delany said. "You'll stay with a senior member for two weeks, after that, you're on your own."

The little girl I had seen in the field was suddenly next to me. "What does that mean?" she asked.

Delany wasn't any nicer to her than she was to the older kids. "You make your own house, find your own food, make your own clothes." It was quiet for a second. "Alright, let's get you guys in houses."

She started to point at people, walk away with them, then come back and do it again. The housing seemed random, whomever Delany pointed at was brought to a house, sometimes close by, sometimes she was gone for a few minutes before coming back for the next person. It took a while, with Delany standing and looking us over as the group got smaller and smaller. I wasn't keeping track, but I'm pretty sure someone snuck away while Delany was gone.

Finally, it was me and the little girl left. Delany had been gone for about two minutes when I introduced myself to her. "I'm Heather," I said, not sure if I should shake her hand. She was little, I didn't know if she knew that yet.

"I'm Byrdie, with a y," she said, looking up at me. "What did you do?"

I hadn't expected her to ask that. I hadn't even thought about it, about why I was there. I frowned. "I don't remember," I said. "Shit."

Before I could even follow that thought, about why I was there in the first place, Byrdie threw me off. "I killed my sister," she said it as if she was talking about the weather. "It was mostly an accident. I didn't mean to drown her, but she died quicker than I thought."

I had no idea what to say to that. This little girl looked so innocent, just looking up at me. Luckily, Delany rounded the corner and looked at Byrdie.

"I have the perfect place for you," she said, though I couldn't tell if she was trying to be sweet or scary. Somehow, I got the feeling it was both.

Delany wasn't gone for long this time. She came back and nodded at me. "You're with me," she said, walking to the closest house. I was wondering why no one had come out of it, peeking, like the other houses had.

Inside, it wasn't as small as it looked. There was a little blanket against the wall, folded out so it looked like a bed, with a pot and a stick leaning against the other. There was a little, frayed black book, clearly years and years old, laying on the bed.

"I don't have another blanket or anything," Delany said, nodding to the opposite wall. There was a folded up—

canvas, maybe? "You can use that as a pillow or a blanket. It itches though, be careful."

Delany sat on her bed and took off her shoes. I followed suit. The ground was cool, compacted dirt. It felt— I didn't know the word for it. Homey.

"Delany," I asked tentatively. She still scared me, even sitting down on my level. "I don't know what I did. I mean, to get here, I don't think I did anything. I just—"

"The drugs they use to transport you guys," she said, futzing with her shoes, "It makes everything fuzzy sometimes. Don't worry, it'll come to you. No one is here without a good reason."

Something about what she said made my stomach churn. I was a decent student, did my chores, fed my cat every day, told my mom I loved her. What could I have done to end up here?

"You know what I was saying about a second?" she said as she put her shoes behind her. I did the same. "I was thinking about you."

"Me?" I asked, looking at her. She looked back at me. Her eyes were a very dark brown, darker than her hair. For once, she looked honest. She looked tired.

"My last second, Angel, she, ugh—well she was forced to make an early departure," Delany said, running her tongue across her lips, like Angel's death was a physical sore spot. "And I can't trust the motherfuckers here, not after that. I need new blood. You're big enough, and Rabbit already likes you, which means he'll get bored soon. You're a good fit." Somehow, I heard an invisible "I think" at the end of her sentence.

"What does being a second mean?" I asked. I leaned against the back wall, and it creaked. I leaned forward again.

"You're like my vice president. If I die, you take over. If I can't go to a meeting, you go. Though you'll probably go to all of them with me anyway. It's easy," she said, shrugging. "You don't have to decide now, you just got here. Give it a day or two. But there is a meeting tonight if you want to get the lay of the land."

I thought for a second. I didn't want to be a second, but if Delany asked, would she be mad if I said no? I figured I could at least go to a meeting, get a better feel for Delany before I decided. Rabbit said she was a sap, maybe it wouldn't be so bad.

"Sure, I'll go," I said, careful not to sound too eager.

"Great," Delany said, though she didn't sound too excited herself. "I'm going to nap. If anything is moved when I wake up, I'll break your neck." She laid down, sighing as she did so. She wasn't bigger than me by more than an inch, and she was practically skin and bone, but I had no doubt that she could.

I laid on my back, trying to process. I was in a prison. A prison with no guards, no supplies, no supervision. There was no way this made any sense. Maybe I died and this is some kind of test, you know? Like, instead of being judged by God, you just get tested one last time, I thought. I didn't know if that was better or worse.

"Hey, kid, get up."

I woke up to Delany shaking my shoulder. I didn't remember going to sleep. I opened my eyes and part of her ragged brown hair was touching me, she was so close.

"Sorry," she said, pulling away from me. "You didn't sound like you were breathing. That happens sometimes, with the drugs. You can't filter them out, or whatever, and it kills you." She almost seemed embarrassed, pulling away from me quickly. "Come on, we have to get to the meeting."

She moved to the other side of the room and started to put her shoes on. I watched her for a second—I could feel her purposefully not looking at me. I stuffed my feet into my sneakers as she stood up. I had no idea what time it was—it occurred to me that I probably wouldn't know what time it was for the foreseeable future. Delany didn't wait for me, she moved the red curtain aside and slipped out. I jumped to my feet to follow her.

The sun was just setting, we had a handful of sunlight left. I had to jog to catch up with Delany. We were the last ones there, but she didn't say anything to me about it. She moved through the building, a woman on a mission, barely making a sound. I was the loudly, gangly child that announce our arrival.

Rabbit smiled when he saw her. "Delany, my dear," he said, offering his hand to her. She let him have it, but rolled her eyes. He kissed her hand, smiling like a fox in the henhouse. "Oh, and you brought the cute one. I knew I could count on you."

Delany ripped her hand away from him. "Everyone, this is Heather," she said as I awkwardly joined them.

"We heard her stomp her way in here," said a black man with pink face paint under his eyes. He seemed annoyed, though he also seemed like he was the kind of person who was always annoyed. I remembered what Delany had said about the Pinks being cannibals, and shivered.

Delany ignored him. "Heather, this is Taver, leader of the Pink, and his second, Pittman." Pittman was a mountain of a man, with arms bigger than me. He was shirtless, with a pink X painted on his chest. He nodded in my direction. I decided I didn't like the Pinks, though I was curious where they were getting paint.

"This is Rue, leader of the Purple," Delany pointed to a—I wasn't sure if they were a man or a woman, but they gave me a friendly smile. "This is Brock, leader of the Green, and Freddie, she's leader of the Blue. Where is Cye?"

"Yeah, we don't know," Rabbit said, his tone making it clear that he knew exactly where Cye was. "Couldn't find her today." Delany gave Rabbit a stern look but didn't say anything about it. I made a note not to spend too much time with Rabbit.

"Did the Orange pick a new leader?" She asked.

"They are discussing it, as we speak," Freddie said, with a little smirk as well. Delany rolled her eyes again.

"Whatever. What do we have to deal with today?" Delany asked, sitting down. Everyone else sat as well. I followed suit.

"Well, with Orange without a leader, they are a bit up in the air at the moment," Brock said, crossing his arms. A big Hispanic looking man, he had more than a few scars up and down his arms. And, as he moved, I realized he was missing two fingers on one hand.

"We aren't fucking with Orange," Rabbit said, sternly, for once. "They have enough trouble as it is."

"They have always been different. I just want to make sure they pick someone who is more in line with our tastes," Freddie said, picking at her nails. They were long and pretty, and she was cleaning dirt out from under them very carefully. "If I were them, I might want revenge."

"No," Delany said, just as sternly as Rabbit. "Rabbit solved that problem. They'll elect someone more agreeable."

Rabbit smiled again, like a proud child.

The way Delany spoke, and how they looked at her, it seemed like she was in charge. Maybe I was wrong, or biased, or just tired, but Delany seemed like she was in charge of all of them. It was the way they looked at her. She was the smallest of them, at least three inches shorter than Freddie and she couldn't have weight more than a hundred pounds, but they listened to her.

Rue cocked their heads to the side. "And you, Delany? How are the newbies? Apparently well, you brought one with you." I could feel myself blushing, and I wasn't sure why.

"Aw, look at her," Freddie said, nudging Rabbit. "So sweet."

"Yeah, we'll fix that soon," Brock said, though it didn't sound very threatening. It sounded more—tired.

Delany ignored them. "There are twenty-six of them. If we're lucky, I think twelve will live."

"What?" I asked, and everyone looked at me. I wasn't sure if I was allowed to speak, but Pittman started to chuckle.

Delany looked like she was going to reach out and touch me, but she stopped. "The drugs kill off a few, the fence gets the ones that try to run. And then that fuckwit that ran into the fence earlier." She huffed, like that way annoying to her.

"Yeah, you have to do something with that body," Freddie said, her nose scrunched up.

"We're not even near you," Delany snapped.

"Still though," Freddie said.

"And then the bats—" Rue started to explain, but Delany started to tell them no.

"Did you not tell them?" Brock asked. "It's always worse when you don't tell them, you know that."

Rabbit caught my eye. "See? A sap, I told you."

"It's their first day, they—" Delany started to say, but Rabbit cut her off. I felt like everyone was talking too fast, or in a different language. I had a friend whose mom would watch Spanish soap operas on TV sometimes, and this felt like that—information I barely understood, presented to me way too quickly.

There was a lull for a second, and Rabbit caught my eye. "We have bats here," he said, his voice soft. "They have some, disease or something. We call it the Plague. One bites you, they swarm and attack you. A week or so later, your skin turns a nasty yellow, and you go insane."

Rue shook their head. "We are barbarians in many ways," they said, "but we kill them before they go crazy. It's for the best, for everyone."

"We burn them," Rabbit clarified. "We don't have any real weapons, and the Plague can spread if it gets too bad. Delany here is a sap, she likes to keep them around until the last second. It's worse that way, but she doesn't listen to us."

Delany didn't look at me, she was looking around the room, as if looking for bats herself.

"Well, there isn't anything Purple needed to talk about," Rue said, standing up. "So unless anyone else has something, I would like to return to my house."

"Who's waiting for you tonight?" Rabbit asked, wiggling his eyebrows at them.

Rue looked like they were going to say something for a second, but they just looked at Rabbit, turn on their heel, and left.

Brock stood up as well. "As long as Red and Orange bury their bodies, we're done too," he said and started to walk away.

"You'll learn," Freddie said as she walked past me, touching the top of my head. Delany swatted her hand away.

"I wouldn't hurt her," Freddie scolded. "She's been here less than twelve hours. We haven't seen the real her yet."

Freddie's eyes widened for a second as she smiled. I decided I didn't like her, either. Pittman and Taver walked away without saying anything.

Delany and Rabbit stood up, so I did the same. "They're all pieces of shit," Delany said to me. "Don't listen to them."

Rabbit offered his arm, though it wasn't clear if it was to me or Delany. "Come on, let me show you the cells. If you're going to be a second, you should see them." I looked at Delany.

"I'll go with you," she said, looking at Rabbit. "I would hate for her to get lost, like Cye." Whatever part Rabbit had played in Cye going missing, Delany clearly wasn't happy about it. I had to say, I wasn't thrilled with the idea either. Being a second was becoming less and less appealing.

Rabbit rolled his eyes. "You slept with her once, you weren't married to her," he said, putting his arm down. "Come on." I followed behind them, stepping exactly where they stepped. I fared better this time, but they were still waiting for me at the door.

I still wasn't sure if I was allowed to ask questions, but I figured it couldn't hurt. "Are all the meetings that short?" I asked.

Delany made a face. "Well, no. We just finished up some stuff, so we are having a bit of a lull." Rabbit smirked. I didn't know what "stuff" was, whether it was Cye or something else, but I had made up my mind. I didn't want to be a second.

We walked in silence. I knew we were moving through different groups, but in the dark, everything looked the same. We walked through the dark, but I could hear bits of conversations, the flapping of flags when the breeze picked up. Had I been anywhere else, it almost would have been romantic, following behind the silhouette of Delany and Rabbit, listening to the crickets.

The building was the dead center of the town, so we hugged the wall as we walked. I could see flickers of light, shadows being thrown around. Finally, we got closer to whatever it was, and I was hit with the yellow light of fire.

Torches were scattered about, lighting up the area. "Why aren't there torches everywhere?" I asked in a whisper. It was so quiet over here, not a hint of conversation. I didn't want to disturb it.

"Bats like them," Delany said, in a whisper as well. "We keep them here because it doesn't matter if the infected get bit again." For some reason, I shuttered.

"It's okay, we'll keep you safe," Rabbit whispered, winking at me. I had no idea if he intended to make me feel better, but he did.

The torches were lighting up cells made of metal. It was clear the people in the prison had made them, they were warped and twisted, and there were parts that were rusted and broken looking. The floors were cement, but other than that, they looked handmade. Inside of them, there were different people. Some of them had clothes, some of them didn't. Rabbit had described them properly—they had sickly looking yellow patches, so bright they seemed to make their own light. Some were worse off than others, ranging from patches so small I hardly noticed them, to looking completely yellow.

As we walked down the line, some of them reached out to us through the bars, crying. Saying they were going to be fine, they didn't feel any different. Towards the end of the line, their skin got more yellow, more covered. Their yelling cut into the silence, making it seem even louder.

"These are Delany's," Rabbit whispered, nodding towards the end of the line. Delany didn't respond. There was a little girl, she must have been six, sitting in her cell, hugging her knees. She reminded me of Byrdie. Half of her face was covered in the Plague, and the tips of her fingers. It might have been the torchlight, but her hair looked silver and wet.

"Delany," the girl said, smiling. "I knew you would come visit." She let go of her knees and crawled towards us. The cages were so small, no one else had much room to move, but she was so little, she could tuck into one corner. Rabbit hung back, letting us go ahead.

"Hi, Michelle. This is Heather," Delany said in a soft voice, introducing me. The girl smiled at me, and I could feel my heart breaking.

"Do you know when it will happen?" Michelle asked, her two little hands around the bars of her cell.

"I talked to Waka and Freddie," Delany said. Her voice was soft; like she was talking to someone she truly cared about. "They don't know, but we think about a week." I hadn't seen Delany like this before, and it made my heart hurt for her.

Michelle's smile fell, and she nodded. She looked at me. "I got bit," she explained, pointing at the yellow patch on her face. "I'm going to go crazy and die soon. Delany is going to burn me."

I looked at Delany. Her eyes looked hollow, like she wasn't really there. "I'll come see you tomorrow, Michelle," she said. Michelle nodded, and crawled back into the corner of her cage. Even Rabbit was quiet.

Michelle was the last in the line of cells, and we started to walk away from them, into the Blue group's area. "When do you do it?" I asked, swallowing a lump in my throat.

"Once a week," Delany said, quietly.

"And you—"

"The group leader kills their own," Rabbit explained for Delany. He was quiet as well, but I could tell this wasn't weight on him like it was on Delany. "It's part of being a leader." That was it for me. I didn't want to be a second. Not if this was part of it.

We walked back to the town hall and hugged it until we got to Yellow. Rabbit said goodbye, reaching out to touch Delany's arm. She pushed him away, hard. He hesitated for a second, then shrugged a little and walked off. Delany and I walked back to Red group quietly. When we got back to her house, she asked me if I believe in God.

"No," I said, honestly.

"Neither do I," she said as she took off her shoes. "Goodnight."

I woke up before Delany the next morning. I knew right away why she slept against the right wall; the sun shone through a hole in the roof and hit the left wall. Specifically, right in my eyes.

I was sweaty and sticky, but considering the bathroom was an open field, I assumed I was going to stay that way. I sat up, and in the daylight, the little house looked a little sadder. The holes in the roof seemed bigger, and the burned wood seems darker. There were people chatting outside, and in the distance, I could hear a bird chirping. It almost seemed pleasant.

I slipped on my shoes and stood in the doorway. We were one of the first houses, so I could see the town hall. It was still dark inside, but it seemed bigger in the daylight. I walked around the house and looked at the rest of the Red group.

People were milling about, leaning out of their houses or sitting on the makeshift streets, talking. I saw a few people I recognized from yesterday talking to the Red group, so I figured they were friendly enough. I even saw Byrdie trying to run her fingers through her hair inside one of the houses. A few people nodded in my direction, and I nodded back.

There was a tap on my shoulder, and I jumped. "Just me," Delany said. Her hair was even more wild than yesterday. "You hungry?" I nodded. "Aren't we all," she said. "Come on, I'll find us something." She went back into the house and came back out with a little pouch. "We've got a big day ahead of us." She walked off, just expecting me to follow her.

"What's that?" I asked, following behind her like a puppy.

"Seeds," Delany said. "I don't have time to grow my own, and either way, Green is really the only place things grow well. I keep the old seeds and sell them back for more food." We kept walking, the town coming to life more and more, getting louder and louder. We walked through a sea of people. I had to be careful to keep up with her. As we walked, two people in Red started to throw punches at each other. Delany watched as we walked past, but did nothing to stop them, or really do anything other than look mildly interested.

We moved from Red into Orange. Had it not been for the color difference, there would have been no way to tell. Their houses looked the same as ours, random and tiny. Orange quickly shifted into Yellow. Yellow's houses were a little bigger, they looked like they could fit two or three people comfortably. As we moved through Yellow, a few people got between us, and I went to reach for Delany's hand, so I wouldn't lose her, but I stopped myself. Instead, I wiggled ahead and got next to her again. She didn't seem to notice

"There's this guy in Yellow," Delany said, in a low voice. Over the sound of everyone else waking up, it was hard to hear. "He has a bit of a crush on me, so I get good deals on stuff. I'll introduce you to him sometime." I wasn't entirely sure I wanted to meet this guy, but I didn't say anything to her about it.

We were walking up on Green now. "You're going to be a second, so you probably won't have time to get food yourself, either," Delany said. She wasn't whispering anymore. We were walking close enough to the cages that we could hear the people screaming; she had to yell over them. "With us, it's always something, you know? So and so stole this, so and so is missing, so and so fought someone from Green and now you have to solve it. You'll have to find ways to get food."

I wasn't sure how to tell Delany that I didn't want to be her second. I wanted to set up a little house, far away from everyone else, and stay there. I didn't want bats, or fighting, or searching for food, or burning people. I wanted to go home.

We made it to Green, and Delany navigated it like she lived there. The houses were placed on a grid system, so it was easy to move around. As we walked, more and more little gardens started to appear on the sides of the houses. Not every house had them, but there were little broken off pieces of wood to mark of gardens, with tiny little plants growing in them. Some didn't have anything but leaves, but some of them had little strawberries, or watermelons, or cucumbers.

We stopped at some little house, and Delany stood in the doorway. "Knock knock," she said, careful not to peek her head in.

"Yeah?" a man's voice said back.

"Your favorite leader, come for breakfast," Delany almost sang. Pittman's appeared. The pink x was gone from his chest; now he had a pink headband tied around his bicep.

"There's my girl," he said, giving her a smile. I hadn't noticed last night, but he was missing a canine tooth on one side. Still, he was an attractive man. I had no idea why he was in a Green house, though.

She handed him the pouch. "Grow something sweet for me, huh?" she said, smiling. Pittman smiled back, reaching over Delany and grabbing someone by the shirt as they walked past.

"Bring this to George," he said, handing them the pouch. They ran off with it. "You and your second hungry?" He moved back into the house.

"Heather," Delany corrected. "And yes."

Pittman was fumbling around for a second, but I couldn't see into the house because Delany had planted herself firmly in the doorway. A few second later, Pittman handed us each what looked like bread.

"Heather," he said, looking me up and down. "I'll have to remember that."

"Excuse me," Delany said, moving slightly in front of me. Pittman gave her a smile.

"You'll always be my favorite," he promised.

"Good," Delany said. She grabbed my hand and led me away, telling me to hide my bread while we walked. "Someone will snatch it right out of your hands." She let go of me once we were out of Green, back on the main road next to town hall.

"I thought he was in Pink?" I said as we walked, careful not to crush the tiny bread in my hand. "Why was he in a Green house?"

"Oh," Delany said, as if she hadn't realized either. "The Pinks are pretty useless here— everyone has their own thing. I'll give you the tour after we deal with that dead guy." I had forgotten about that, the guy who ran into the fence. I had never seen a dead body before.

Back in our house, Delany practically threw herself onto the floor. "Ugh," she said, fishing her bread out of her dirty pocket. "I'm not a morning person." She brushed it off, which didn't seem to do anything, and took a bite. "Go on," she said, her mouth full. "It's bad, but you get used to it. Pitt is one of the few people here who can keep it from growing mold."

I took a bite. She was right, it was bad. It tasted like he had used sand instead of flour. "I thought you said seconds didn't have time to make food," I said, struggling to swallow it. It felt like sandpaper grinding down my throat. I would have killed for some water.

"You won't. Pitt doesn't even make this himself," she said, "His husband does."

I shook my head. "I thought—" I started to say.

"Nope," she said quickly. "He's very dedicated to George."

I finished the last bite of my bread. "How long have you been here?" I asked. It occurred to me I had no idea how old Delany was. She looked a few years older than me, but that wasn't saying much.

"I've been here for my whole life," Delany said, licking a crumb off her finger. "My mom got pregnant when she was here, died giving birth to me." She said it like it was nothing. "When I was really little, I used to trade whatever I had to hear people tell stories of the outside."

I wanted to ask her more, how her mom got pregnant, if she knew her father, who took care of her, how— Delany stood up. "Come on, time to go deal with the dead guy."

Turns out, dealing with a dead guy is not fun. Delany got another Red to help his, she called him Socks. The three of us walked out all the way to the fence. Delany said it was about a mile and a half, but it felt a lot longer. We went all the way out there, then walked the fence line until we found his body.

He was about three feet away from the fence, covered in flies. I hadn't recognized him, a boy with long black hair. I had thought that people looked peaceful when they died. His eyes were open, his mouth as well. He almost looked like a cartoon character after they get shocked.

A fly crawled out of his mouth. "Fucking nasty," Socks said, shaking his head. "How long as he been out here?"

"Since yesterday, around mid-afternoon," Delany said, looking at the dead body. There was a fly on his eyeball, and I rubbed both of my eyes. "That's the problem with me not having a second, I can't keep track of all you idiots myself."

"I'm not the idiot who ran into an electric fence," Socks pointed out.

"Yeah, but you're the idiot who agreed to help me bury him," Delany said, sweetly. Socks mimicked her words back at her. "Come on, help me grab him."

I wanted to ask Delany what she wanted me to do, but honestly, I didn't want to help. Delany lifted him by his shoulders, and Socks grabbed his feet, and they carried him.

"Where are we taking him?" I asked as we walked. I walked a few feet away from them, off to the side. The flies that had covered his body were following us now, like the world's smallest funeral procession.

"By the cages," Delany huffed. "We have a— Socks, what do you guys call them?"

"Mass grave," Socks said.

"We have a mass grave back there were we throw people," she said.

We walked all the way over to the cages, I had no idea how far it was. It was getting hotter and hotter as the day moved on, and they had to stop sometimes to readjust. When we got close, Delany told Socks to stop. They put the boy back on the ground, and Delany pointed at me. "You take him," she said, using the back of her hand to wipe the sweat off her forehead.

"Delany—" I didn't know what to say. She moved away from his shoulders, and feeling like I didn't have another option, I took her place. He was heavier than I expected, and hard to hold. I had no idea how she had done it for so long.

We moved the last little bit to the cages, and I saw what she meant. There was a pile of dirt, maybe four feet tall, but about twenty feet long. Next to it, a long trench.

"Orange must have gotten her last night," Socks said as he and I moved closer to the edge. There was fresh dirt laid down. I looked over at Delany. She had stayed back, not wanting to come close. Socks counted us down, and we swung the body into the trench.

"You can cover him, I'm leaving," Socks said to me, then looked at Delany. "Next one who kills themselves is your problem, it's too fucking hot for this shit."

Delany didn't say anything as he walked away, and she didn't say anything after he was gone. She was just looking around, like she was waiting for something. I put my hands in the dirt and started to push as much of it as I could on top of the boy.

It took me maybe forty minutes to cover him to what I thought was a respectable level. Once I had finished, I walked over to Delany. "You good?" she asked me. I nodded. "Good."

As promised, Delany showed me my new world.

We walked through the grass back to Red. Red was home now. It didn't feel like it, but I felt slightly less tense when I was there. I recognized some of their faces. Not that that mattered; everyone had some kind of red on them. Two girls, who could have been twins, had red string braided into their hair. Delany had a red scrap of cloth tied to a belt loop in her jeans. Another girl had what looked like red mud in a heart on her face. A boy, I think his name was Timmy, had a red shirt. Delany told me that new people would be offered things for their clothing if it matched another group.

We went through Red and into Orange. Orange was next to us, a few of their houses even leaned against ours. "Cloth," Delany told me as we walked into the Orange area. "They have a small patch where cotton grows, right back there." Delany pointed down a row of houses, towards a patch of grass I could barely see. "It was here when we got here, and Orange got it. Takes them forever, but it's all they got."

"And they can turn it into actual cloth here?" I asked. I had learned in school about cotton picking, and the cotton wheel or gin or whatever it was called, but for a place made out of nothing, being able to make cloth impressed me.

"A very well guarded secret," Delany said with a little shrug. "It's one of the few luxury items here."

We walked along. Orange never bothered me much. They were so close to us, and without a leader, there was no one to be afraid of. Besides, Delany was friendly with a few of them, so people nodded as we walked by.

Yellow was next. I thought I should feel welcome there—Rabbit had been very welcoming, I guess. Something about walking through it though made my hair stand on end. I think it was how the sound traveled there—they had set their houses so close together, you could never tell which direction noises were coming from. I felt like people were either yelling or whispering there.

A bit of yellow cloth flapped in the wind. Delany and I looked at it as we passed. It occurred to me that she was born here, this was all she knew of the world. I could feel my chest tighten. I couldn't image—everyone else was so proud of their group, their color. It was like a badge, a family. I knew Red was my place now, but to her, it was everything. This place was everything.

Yellow faded into Green. Food, I thought as we walked by. Delany didn't have to say it. Green's houses were more spaced out, so I could see the little gardens as we walked by. I saw Pittman standing by one of them, guarding what looked like watermelons, barely the size of my pinky. Delany nodded down one of the little roads, and I looked.

A massive man, his arms crossed, was sitting in front of another garden. He had a pink bandana around his head.

"Green's hire out Pinks to guard their food," Delany said. "Pinks don't fuck with Greens, as long as the Green's pay up."

"Nice system they got going here," I said as we walked along. It looked like another garden was growing strawberries. I remembered how my mom went through a phase were she wanted to eat only raw, vegan food. She had tried to convince me to do it with her.

"Until there's not enough food," Delany said. "We lost about ten Greens not too long ago in that fight." *We.* I was right. All of this was her home, not just Red. I got why Rabbit called her a sap.

Between Blue and Green, the cages sat. As we walked by, the people inside of them howled. Delany wouldn't look in that direction. She didn't say anything, but she started to walk a little faster. I didn't mind.

Blue was quite, except for the piercing cry of a baby. I looked at Delany. "I have no idea whose it is, but it's not going to last long," Delany said with a sigh. "They never do."

"You did," I said.

"I'm the exception." She didn't say it proudly, she said it like it was a burden. I reached out to take her hand, then stopped myself.

"Water," Delany said, changing the subject. "Blue has water, the only well we have."

Blue's houses were set up to be centered around the well. While everyone else had thrown together a house where ever they could, and wore down the earth to make paths between them, Blue had had a plan, for the most part. Their older houses, the ones closest to the well, were orderly. They were set up in a circle around it so that the houses made a barrier for it. You couldn't look at the well from the main road, you had to weave in between houses to get to it. I didn't blame them.

"Luckiest fuckers here," Delany said as we started to weave through houses. There were only three circles of houses before you got to the well. Freddie was standing there, with some other Blues.

"Delany," she said with a smile. "What brings you here?"

"I'm thirsty," Delany said.

"What have you got for me?" Freddie asked, crossing her arms.

"Me not kicking your ass?" Delany offered. A few Blue's chuckled, but Freddie didn't flinch. I had seen fights in high school, two boys arguing over a girl, two girls arguing over homework— I had never seen anyone really fight. I glanced at Delany. She was skin and bone, barely thick enough to keep from blowing away in the wind. I couldn't imagine her lasting long in a fight.

"You owe me," Delany said. "From last time."

"Blue doesn't owe you anything," Freddie said. A few of the Blue's moved to be closer to her. I could feel my heart race. I had never been in a fight before. I didn't even have any siblings to play fight with.

"Blue doesn't. You do," Delany corrected. "Freddie, you don't want to start this."

They looked at each other for what felt like an eternity. I was becoming increasingly aware that while the houses blocked people from the well, it also blocked people from the main road. I would have to weave in and out of them to get any kind of help, past how many Blues.

Freddie cracked a smile and laughed. "I love messing with you, come here," she said, leaning over the well and pulling up an old, slimy rope. At the end of it, a small, metal bucket appeared. It looked like someone had tried to crush it once; one side was almost completely caved in.

Delany stepped forward and took the bucket. She cupped her dirty hand and put it inside, scooping up water and bringing it to her mouth. When she was done, she nodded to me. I did the same, trying to get as much water as I could with each scoop. It wasn't a lot.

Delany tapped my leg with two fingers, and I stopped. "Thank you," Delany said with a sweet smile. Freddie smiled back.

"We're even, Red."

Purple always felt so much bigger than the other colors. They had the biggest houses, two or three people fit comfortably there. "They got all the materials when we got here," Delany said, clearly envious. "Now they break down stuff, find things to build with, and sell them off."

Purple was my favorite color, but it wasn't much to see. Their bigger houses seemed huge in comparison, but a few weeks ago, I would have thought they were outhouses.

The Purples hung around and played games. It looked sort of like chess, but with fewer rules, but not quite checkers. Delany promised she would teach me, later.

Pink was the smallest, by far. While the other colors it was hard to tell how many people were there, Pink was easy. About 25. Their houses stood crooked and empty. They took everything with them when they went to work. I was almost jealous of the Pinks. They were the biggest, the scariest, so they got all of the jobs. I wish I had something to do during the day, but I wasn't scary enough to fit in. And I wasn't into the whole cannibalism thing.

A small archway separated Pink and Red. It was clearly meant to be an entrance, but no one used it as such. I hadn't seen anyone use it for more than an empty space to hang out in.

"Delany," I said, and she stopped. The archway had people under it, playing something that looked similar to marbles, but with balled up pieces of grass. "Has anyone taught you anything about the outside world?"

She looked, annoyed, or maybe embarrassed. "Of course," she snapped.

"Do you know who the president is?" It was the first question that came to mind.

"Does it matter?"

"No."

"Then no."

She started to walk again. "No, but really," I said. "I could teach you. I did graduate high school. I could tell you about plants, and history, and stars, and—"

Delany stopped in her tracks. "Is that going to keep me fed? Give me water? Help me stay warm?"

"No, but it's something to do," I said. "What else do we have to do all day?"

"I don't know about you, but I have real things to worry about," Delany snapped. She took a few steps, and I started after her. She put her arm out to block me. "Get lost."

Delany went into the town hall, and with nothing better to do, I followed her, careful to be a few feet behind her. Red was nearly empty when we walked through it, a few people walking around on what looked like a patrol, but other than that, nothing.

She marched straight into the town hall, right into the center, and yelled for everyone's attention. I caught up, but moved towards the back. She clearly wanted space from me, I wanted some space from her, too.

Delany was speaking like she was teaching a class. Someone had already died because of the drugs, and Delany was having someone take his things and toss the body out. People asked her how they were supposed to eat, what they were supposed to do in their free time. She answered everything shortly, but directly. I was only half listening to her.

The other people around, the older Reds, were talking about us. Guessing what we did, how long we would last. A few people were placing bets. I listening to them for a while, but I had this aching feeling in my stomach, and it wasn't from breakfast. Something wasn't right. I knew I wasn't supposed to be here, that I didn't do anything. But Delany said no one was here without a good reason.

I took a psychology class in high school and we talked about how people repress things. I think it was something Freud had said. My teacher always said that Freud was full of shit because there was no way to prove his theories wrong, he would claim you just repressed whatever happened. But maybe he was right. Maybe I did something horrible and repressed it. Or maybe I was right, and this was an awful coma dream.

I closed my eyes and decided to really and truly focus on what I remembered before I woke up in the field. I don't know how long I stood there, eyes closed, before something came to me. I remember hitting my head on something metal. I don't even think my eyes were open, because I don't remember seeing anything. Just the clash of my head hitting metal, and someone moving my head away. A gloved hand.

I opened my eyes and caught sight of Rabbit sneaking by. He was lurking behind some machine, listening to Delany talk. She was busy moving machinery, trying to explain how not to get crushed. I looked back at Rabbit and he waved me over.

"Hey," he whispered as I walked over. "I thought you were a goody-two-shoes and wouldn't come over."

"I ended up here, didn't I?" I bluffed.

Rabbit looked impressed. "Come here." He took my hand and pulled me through a hole in the wall. "Voices carry in there." He looked me up and down. "So, how's it going in Hell?" he asked, playfully.

I didn't know how to answer him. "It's going? I guess?" I said. He crossed his arms.

"Everyone here is a criminal, you need to learn how to lie better," he said, frowning. "It's like that book, that really old one. With the people stuck on the island." I didn't know what he was talking about. "Anyway, it's every man for themselves. I know we're in groups, but that doesn't mean shit. And sadly, you got stuck with a sap."

"You keep saying that," I said, looking at him. Really looking. He had crust in his eyes still, his hair was pressed down on one side from when he was sleeping. It looked like he had woken up in a hurry. "What do you mean?"

"She has a hard time killing her people. She's very emotional," Rabbit said, leaning against the brick wall. It barely seemed stable enough to hold him up, but he didn't move. "She isn't good at punishing people. Her second, Angel—well I guess her old second now—"

"I'm not her second," I corrected. I wasn't sure what had gotten into me. Delany scared me, but Rabbit? He seemed harmless. A bit of a jackass, but harmless.

Rabbit raised an eyebrow. "Oh, cause she's telling people you are." I frowned. "Either way, her last second had to be killed off by Purple because she wouldn't do it."

"Why? Why did she *have* to be killed?" I asked, crossing my arms.

"Oh, you sweet, little child," Rabbit said, very condescendingly. "We still have rules here. No stealing, to a degree, no killing, to a degree, no raping, no—well, that's really it. She was stealing left and right, honestly, it's a miracle she didn't die in a fist fight, and she might have killed off a few people she wasn't supposed to."

"What?" I asked, not even sure where to start with my questions.

"We have a justice system, here," Rabbit said. "She broke the rules, we all agreed. It wasn't like she stole two or three things to survive. She was being a real bitch about it. Delany wouldn't do anything about it. She had a bit of a crush on her. She tends to, with her seconds."

"What the fuck is wrong with you people?" I asked, uncrossing my arms so I could wave them at him. "Are you all just wrong in the head?"

"You put a whole bunch of, well, mostly, teenagers in a confined place with no supervision and the threat of a painful death? Yeah, things are gonna go to shit, kid. We aren't all just gonna get together and share, okay?" Rabbit said, as if it was very obvious. "Listen, if this is too much for you, the fence is a quick death."

"No," I said, sharply. Rabbit looked me up and down again. "I had to deal with that this morning."

"What did you do, anyway, Heather?" He looked at me like he really wanted to know, and right then, I really wanted to tell him. But I still didn't remember. From my silence, he seemed to gather that. "If you don't know, here's a tip. Lie. Pittman used to fight dogs, which is how he got his name. No one took him seriously here until he cracked a few skulls. We are in a shit ass prison, for the worst of the worst. Even if you aren't, pretend you are." Rabbit pat me on the shoulder. "You should get back in there, kid."

"Wait," I said as I pulled away from his touch. "Why do you keep talking to me? There's a bunch of new people. Why me?"

He shrugged. "Delany took interest in you, which means she sees something. Even if Angle was a bad pick, she got shit done while she was around. Delany knows what she's doing, so if she likes you, there's something to it." He looked around, as if to make sure no one was listening to him. "Shit gets crazy around here, and whether Delany likes it or not, we're on the same side."

He put his hand on my shoulder and nudged me back towards the hole in the wall. I looked at him for a second, then went back inside.

If Delany had noticed I was missing, she didn't say anything. She was wrapping up whatever she was saying, sitting down on a busted table. I saw Byrdie sitting alone, pushing some loose dirt around. I went to go sit next to her.

"Did you eat this morning?" I asked, trying not to sound concerned.

"Yeah, the guy I'm staying with fed me," Byrdie said. "Whatever it was tasted terrible."

I didn't like the idea of her staying with a man, but I guess there wasn't much I could do about it, aside from building my own house and letting her stay with me. Even with the interest in me, I was still a ways away from that. "Is he nice?" I asked her, leaning against some machine part.

"He's fine," Byrdie said, though I don't know if she realized what I was fishing at. *Delany is a sap*, I repeated to myself. *There is no way she would put a child with someone dangerous.*

Brydie didn't seem to want to talk, and I didn't either. I wanted to go home, to be alone for a little while. I looked across the room at Delany. She was talking loudly about fights, and who we were allowed to fight with. I didn't care. I didn't care about any of this. I didn't care about groups, or dead people by fences, or eating, or bats, or what group got to sit in the stupid town hall.

I stood up and started to walk towards the front door. I heard Delany yell out something, but I didn't turn. I left and went back to her house, sitting on the floor by myself, trying not to scream.

I sat in the house alone for maybe four hours. I had never really been alone with my thoughts for that long before. I always had a TV, or a book, or someone to talk to, just something. But sitting there, on the floor with nothing, I had to think things through.

Delany is already telling people I'm her second. I was pissed about that, but Delany was also taking care of me, so how much of a right did I have to be mad? What was I going to do, run off and try to sleep in a field by myself? Rabbit said there was a justice system here, but I didn't trust it enough to leave what little protection Red seemed to offer.

Rabbit told me she's a sap, but she doesn't seem to give a shit about anything. She walked a dead body a mile and barely batted an eye. Even Socks seemed a little upset. Or even grossed out. But she's lived here her whole life, maybe she's just cold because she doesn't know any better. Like a kid raised by wolves. Or maybe she's a psychopath.

I had no idea what to think about anything. Everyone seemed insane, in their own special ways. I was pretty sure I didn't like anyone, even Delany. I didn't want to be her second, but I also didn't want her to throw me out. Besides, she also had access to food. I wasn't really in a place where I could leave her.

It started to get darker, and I heard people talking outside. I figured everyone was heading back home for the night, and I stuck my head out of the house. People wandered past. Someone bit into a strawberry, and the sight of it made my mouth water so badly I almost drooled. I wiped my mouth with the back of my hand and realized I had nothing to eat all day, aside from a shitty piece of bread, and worse, almost nothing to drink. Reluctantly, I left the house and went back into the town hall, looking for Delany.

"Delany, you can't," a woman said in a harsh whisper. "She's my only child."

The sun was setting, but I could see Delany's face clearly. She had that faraway look again. I thought I saw her lip quiver, but she bit it right after.

"Sandy, I'm sorry," Delany said, not meeting her eye. "I know, its—"

"You don't know anything," the woman said, loudly now. So loud it seemed to echo. "You've never lost a child." Delany seemed to wince, even though the woman didn't even raise a hand. She turned and stormed off, pushing past me, though she didn't need to. The other people around Delany started to wander off as well.

"You okay?" I asked her as I walked over. She looked like she was about to cry.

Delany looked up at me, and the look was gone. Her face was pure steel, not a hint of the tears she had in her eyes moments before. "I'm fine, why?" she asked, then shook her head. "Come on, we have to go."

"Go where?" I asked as I followed her. We didn't leave out of the main door, we walked to the other end and wiggled out of a smaller hole. Delany didn't bother answering me. We were out in front of the cages, the torches were being lit as we came out of the town hall. "Are you—" I couldn't say it. "Tonight?"

Delany took in a deep breath and looked at me, but didn't say anything. I didn't know if she even wanted to. Rue walked over and said hello before she got a chance. "Excited?" they asked me, a small smile on their face. "We had to move this up, you know. It wasn't supposed to happen for a few days, but with more people, we attract more bats, and well, we are running low on cages."

Rue seemed shorter now, I don't know if it was the lighting or the setting. They were wrapped in cloth, it looked new, or newer. They had a purple star painted on their cheek, the purple standing out against their light brown skin. "You should be," Rue said, and I almost forgot what we were talking about.

Rue walked away and stood next to Brock. I heard Rabbit before I saw him, practically jumping up and down with part of Yellow. There was a general buzz of excitement in the air, like this was some kind of sporting event. People were gathering quickly.

I looked at Delany. I watched her, watching everyone else. She was completely expressionless.

"How do you know her?" I asked, following Delany's eyes. They were on Michelle's cage.

"She's my cousin," Delany said, then swallowed hard. "Sandy is my aunt." I felt a shiver run up my spine.

"And we're sure there's nothing we can do for her?" I asked, when someone in one of the other cages screamed. Once they stopped, everyone let out a laugh. "For them?" I corrected.

"Not with what we have," Delany said.

I repeated my old question. "Are you going to— " I still couldn't say it. Delany looked at me.

"It would be better if I did, wouldn't it?" she asked, and I mean genuinely asked. She wasn't just asking my opinion, she was asking a real question.

"I—I don't know," I stammered. If I had said yes, would she be angry? Even more than that, did I really think it was okay to kill a sick child?

Delany and I were quiet, standing against the brick wall, watching everyone else enjoy their night. Even people from the Red group started to show up and mingle. Eventually, Rabbit bounced over to us.

He held out a fist to Delany, and she shook her head. "Come on, it's a holiday," he said, pushing his hand closer to her. "And a gift. It'll make you feel better."

"No," Delany said sternly. "Get lost."

Rabbit held out his hand to me. "You got a habit?" he asked.

"What?" I asked Delany.

"He's offering you drugs," Delany said. "I don't know why you try to be sneaky about it, Jack, there's no one here that'll stop you."

"Yeah, but I might take a crack to the back of the skull for it," Rabbit said. He moved his hand closer to me. "You want?"

"No, I'm good, thanks," I said. "How did you even get that?"

Rabbit shrugged. "Some of us have friends on the outside. I get drugs, Pittman gets food, Taver gets booze." Rabbit smiled. "If you want something, let me know, I'll help you out." Delany didn't have to say it this time, he skipped away on his own, but not before winking at the two of us.

"So that's why he's like that?" I asked, and Delany let out a chuckle.

"Yeah. He thinks he's hot stuff because he befriended a guard," Delany said, rolling her eyes. "We used to see them, when they dropped people off. Now, if we get too close, they give us a dart in the neck too. They still bring stuff, though."

"What does Rabbit give them in return?" I asked, watching him. He shook hands with someone from Red group, who smiled at him. I couldn't imagine what he had to offer a guard.

"His family is rich," Delany said. "I don't know what the others do for their stuff, but I know Rabbit's family pays them off." She shook her head. "All the money in the world, and he's still starved half to death like the rest of us."

"That's his problem," I said, watching him. He pulled something out of his back pocket and put it in his mouth. "He could be getting food in here if he wanted." I felt Delany's eyes on me, so I looked at her.

"He's a good kid," she said, though it almost seemed like she was reassuring herself. "We're all trying out best."

I expected people to start gathering wood or something—we were going to burn people, after all. No one did, though, they all stood around chatting, laughing. I think some kids were playing tag or something. No one talked to us, though some people did wave.

"They moved this up?" I asked Delany. She nodded. "Did they talk to you about it?" There were fourteen cages, two for each group. Red only had one person, but twelve of the cages were full.

"No."

"Why not?"

"Didn't have to. We are running out of cages. Doesn't matter what I think about it." She had been looking at the ground for the last couple of minutes, but now she looked up at everyone again. Everyone in the entire prison had to have been there, maybe three hundred people. It was like a party, with someone beating a drum or something, people dancing, laughter. If I hadn't known what was happening, it would have been fun.

Eventually, it seemed like an hour had passed, Rue and Brock moved toward the cages. Rabbit skipped up there with them, rolling his head around like he was warming up for a fight. Everyone got quiet as they moved towards the cages.

"Friends," Rue said, and I looked at Delany, figuring she should be up there too. She didn't move. "We are here today to end the suffering of our own." The crowd cheered, as if we had won something. Rue held up a hand to quiet them down.

"First, we say goodbye to the Yellows," Rue said, and again, people cheered. Rabbit jumped up and got a torch, practically giddy. He walked over to the first cage, all smiles. The person inside of it was long gone, screaming and banging around the cage. They seemed more animal than human. Delany and I were far enough back that I couldn't smell him as he burned, but I could hear him scream. Rabbit moved out of the way so everyone could see. I still couldn't. People cheered.

The second person in line was still all there, still a person. She cried and promised to run into the fence. She wailed. Rabbit didn't even flinch. He stuck the torch in the cage, and she started to burn. People cheered.

"Can we leave?" I asked.

"No."

Someone else was screaming as Rabbit lit them on fire. People cheered.

I didn't know why she wanted to say. She wasn't up there, so I figured she wasn't going to kill Michelle tonight. Why did we have to stay? The other leaders who weren't killing anyone weren't there. Why did we have to be?

Rabbit had one more person to kill. I tried to remember back to last night, to seeing them. I didn't remember how far gone he was. As Rabbit moved closer, he didn't say anything, didn't cry. He screamed when Rabbit touched him with the torch, but he died quickly, and compared to the others, quietly. Almost like he had practiced beforehand. People cheered.

Rabbit skipped back to the front and handed Brock the torch, bowing as he did so. Brock leaned in, like he was saying something to Rabbit, but we were too faraway to hear. Delany's mouth moving caught the corner of my eye and I peeked at her. Whatever they had said, she mouthed along with them.

"And now we say goodbye to the Greens," Rue announced. There was another cheer.

Brock moved to his first cage. He stopped, and though I wasn't sure, I wanted to believe he was apologizing to her. She wailed and cried as well, calling him out by name. She died yelling "Brock!" over and over again. The second girl he killed died the same way, screaming his name. And the third. And the fourth. And the fifth. People cheered.

The smell was becoming overwhelming. The entire town smelt, like body-odor, rot, and death, but the smell of burning flesh seemed to be a thousand times worse. As Brock walked back to the front and handed Rue his torch, I tapped Delany.

"Can I leave?" I asked quietly, starting to feel nauseous.

"No."

"And now, the Purple," Rue said. This time, they didn't seem as excited. They walked slowly, holding the torch carefully. They only had two people. As they moved, I caught sight of little Michelle in the next cage over. My heart broke for her, having to watch her fate play out before her like that.

Rue paused as well, and again, I liked to think they was saying something nice. This person too, yelled and screamed. I didn't remember their gender, and their screams were no help. They burned both people quickly, one right after the other, so their screams and smoke mixed together. People cheered.

Rue was standing back at the front, the line of burning bodies illuminating the crowd of people. He was looking directly at Delany, even though we were as far away as we could have been. He held out the torch, waiting. Delany didn't move.

They both stared each other down. It almost felt like they were having a conversation. People started to yell things like "Come on" and "just do it already" while others booed. Over their yells, I heard Delany sigh. She took a step forward, and I went to follow her.

I walked with Delany up to the cages, the crowd parting and cheering as we went. I wanted to throw up. I stopped at the edge of the crowd, letting Delany go up to the cages herself. The smell was worse now, so strong I felt like I couldn't breathe. I could feel the heat of the fire, the smoke was swirling above me. I could see the charred bodies, still burning. They didn't look like people, but like monsters. I gagged, putting my hand over my mouth, forcing the nothing that was in my stomach to stay there.

Delany walked up to Rue and grabbed the torch forcefully. I couldn't hear her, but I could see her mouth something that looked like "Fuck you."

People cheered as she touched the torch, the Reds loudest of all. She walked over to Michelle and I watched Rabbit rock back and forth, so quickly it seemed like he was going to take off. I watched him instead of her.

Delany must have been talking to Michelle because there was a good while before I heard her scream. I watched Rabbit the whole time, rocking back and forth, back and forth. The smile he had had on his face was gone now, replaced by a far away stare. I couldn't tell if it was because of the drugs or remorse.

Delany didn't wait around. She handed Rue back the torch and walked back into the crowd, Michelle still screaming. They parted as she moved away from them, and I followed behind her. As we walked away, over the screaming, Rue said, "We say goodbye to those we have lost."

People cheered.

Part Two

I don't know what time it was, but I knew it was early in the morning. I woke up to the sound of dry heaving. It was dark, but I could make out the outline of Delany, half in the house half out, on her hands and knees. Without thinking, I moved next to her and held her hair.

"Get off of me," she said, pushing me away. I fell back into the wall, almost caving the whole house in on us.

"Delany, I— "

"Shut up," she snapped, sitting up and wiping her mouth. "If you tell anyone, I swear by all that is holy, I'll—"

"Maybe we can do something," I suggested, "Ask the others if we could let them run into the fence, so they can die quickly. I don't think Rue or Brock like doing this either, and Rue, he—or she?"

Delany ran the back of her hand across her mouth again. "Depends on the day."

"Whatever. Maybe we can get them to stop," I said. I could hear her breathing.

"They aren't going to," she said finally. "It's tradition." Her voice sounded as defeated as I felt.

"We can try," I said, trying to sound sure of myself. Delany didn't say anything. She crawled back over to her bed and laid down, her back to me. We were quiet for a while, and I figured she had fallen asleep. I was almost asleep myself when I heard her, in a voice lower than a whisper, say "thank you."

The next morning, we woke up to rain. Delany was gone when I woke up, doing I don't know what. I wasn't about to go wander around in the rain to find her. The holes in the roof were already letting enough water in.

I sat in the house until I noticed Reds starting to move towards town hall. The rain had slowed then, so I followed them. The hall was only a bit drier, and I noticed there were a few Pinks and Blues hanging around, I'm assuming to stay dry. Delany was in there already, and today, she wasn't chasing anyone out.

While we sat around, I thought about my science class. In third grade, we raised baby chicks from eggs, then gave them to a farm. I don't think they lasted long there, we were probably eating them for dinner a few months later. I felt like that, too. My entire life so far was going from egg to chick, where people cared about me and made sure I was fed and had fun. Now, I was on the farm, waiting to become a meal for someone else.

Someone tapped me on the shoulder. I jumped, and somehow resisted the urge to scream. I turned quickly. A small girl was holding two hands up, as if trying to calm a scared horse.

"Hey, sorry, wow," she said, hands still raised. "I didn't think you were going to do that."

She was in Green. Her dirty and matted, muddy colored hair was braided on the side, a dirty piece of green cloth weaved into the braid. She was cute though, with a round face and full cheeks, or cheeks that would have been full compared to everyone else there. Brown eyes blinked at me.

"What's up?" I asked, taking in a breath. My heart was beating out of my chest.

She looked up at me innocently. She must have been around my age, but I was half a foot taller than her. "Nothing, Brock just said we should be nice to the new Reds. I thought maybe I would show you around."

Something about the way she said it made my skin crawl. "Oh yeah?" I asked, trying to sound calm. I threw a glance back at Delany. She was laying on one of the tables, looking up at nothing.

"She won't mind," the girl said.

I wanted to say that I wasn't worried about that, I was worried about whatever it was that happened to Delany's second before me. "Sure," I said, feeling a little better that we would have to walk through Yellow to get to Green. Maybe I could grab Rabbit's attention somehow, if I needed him.

She smiled at me. "Perfect," she said, "Oh, I'm Cassidy, by the way."

"Heather."

"Oh, I know."

There was something about her that was off. She was too chipper, but not like Rabbit. It was a fake happiness, something about her that screamed she was trying too hard. Even as she turned around to leave the building, the way she stepped, the way her hair bounced, there was something off about it.

I followed her out of the building, then walked next to her. She chatted a bit, telling me about how it was always "just so exciting" to get new people. As we walked into Yellow, I slowed down.

"You know, can I make a quick pit stop? I wanted to talk to a friend real quick," I said, stopping in the little walkway.

"Oh, yeah, totally," she said, her voice bleeding with this fake enthusiasm. "You make friends fast, huh?" She let out a fake little laugh.

"Yeah," I said, then quickly ducked into the first Yellow house that had a person in it.

It was small, just like Delany's. The person in it, a small boy with short hair, looked up at me from the floor. "What the fuck do you want?" he asked.

"Hey, I need a favor," I said. Before I could even finish, he stood up.

"Who the fuck are you?" he said, practically spitting at me.

"Be quite," I said, more concerned with his volume than his tone. "You need to tell Rabbit that Heather is in Green. Now."

"Why the fuck—"

"You need to tell him now."

I was trying to be like Delany, tough and commanding. I wasn't sure if I was pulling it off. This was probably the most direct I had been in my life. I felt like I was in a school play, trying to harness some kind of power I never had before. The boy didn't look impressed. Honestly, I wasn't either.

"Fine," he finally said, looking me up and down.

I turned to leave, but remembered to throw in a quick thank you before doing so. Back outside, it was starting to drizzle again. I walked over to Cassidy and smiled. "Thanks! Alright, back to the tour!" I tried not to sound as fake as she had, but again, I don't think I was pulling it off.

She smiled back at me, but didn't say anything. We walked forward.

Green probably had the most color representation on its houses. Little scraps of cloth draped over doorways and windows, and paint ranging from neon green to a green so dark it almost looked brown.

"They used to give us stuff," Cassidy said. "It was before I got here. We used to get like cloth, and like, um, shoes and stuff like that, you know? They stopped after a while, which is like, whatever, but I guess it makes us appreciate what we have, you know?" She let her hand touch a piece of green fabric as we walked. "It's like a big deal to us."

"Yeah," I said, "I bet."

"Oh, you know what you would love? We all have like, these little gardens. We have the best area for it, which is like, so lucky. Come on, I'll show you." She took a turn, and I followed her, trying to keep tracks of what lefts and rights we made.

Cassidy stopped when we got to the edge of the houses. I could see the fence in the distance. It looked taller and darker in the rain. "This is where all the good stuff is," Cassidy said. Out directly in front of us were a few decent sized plants, and a bunch of smaller ones. Some of them were so small, I wasn't completely sure they weren't just weeds.

"Why are you showing me this?" I asked, turning to look at her. She looked offended that I would even ask.

"I'm just showing you what Green has to offer," she said, looking at the plants. "We grow a decent bit of food, you know. Some berries, or like a potato or two, you know."

Most of the food had to be brought in by the guards, I had figured that out by now. There was no way anyone here could grow any kind of wheat for flour, and yet most of us were eating bread. "Uh-huh," I said, looking at her. "I'm going to head back now."

I couldn't tell if Cassidy was upset or angry with me. "Do you want me to walk you back?" she asked. Her tone didn't help me figure it out.

"No," I said shortly.

Most of the Reds had left when I got back. In fact, there were only maybe ten people hanging around. I found Delany where I had left here, sitting on the table. Rue was standing in front of her. I walked up slowly, not wanting to intrude, but she waved me over.

Rue paused as I walked up. "This is the only entertainment they have," Rue said, looking at me. "We can't take it away from them."

"I'm not," Delany said, very matter of fact. "They can watch you burn people."

Rue didn't look happy, but they had nothing else to say. They let out a little huff and walked away. Delany turned to look at me. "Rue's not a fan of my choices," she said, as if it wasn't obvious.

"What did you say to them yesterday?" I asked.

"Where were you?" she asked, as if I hadn't said anything.

"Some Green pulled me aside, Cassidy," I said shaking my head. "She wanted to show me the garden? It was weird."

"Cassidy?" Delany repeated.

"Yeah." It wasn't me that spoke. Without even seeing him, it was clear that it was Rabbit. He walked out from behind a machine.

"Do you just lurk around here?" Delany asked, crossing her arms.

"No, I followed her back," Rabbit said, nodding towards me. Delany shot me a look. "I got Scotty's message. Good call on that." Delany kept looking at me, but I couldn't tell if she was impressed or annoyed. After a second, she looked back at Rabbit. "It was fine," Rabbit said, answering a question she didn't ask. "Nothing sketchy, girls just a fucking creep." Delany nodded.

"What's the plan for today?" Delany asked, leaning her elbows on her knees. "I heard Noel got picked for Orange."

"Yeah," Rabbit said, going to sit down next to her. "She's a good pick." Delany nodded. "Do you wanna talk about— "

"No."

Rabbit nodded silently. He looked at me for a second, raised his eyebrows, then lowered them. I gave him a little nod.

We sat in silence for a few minutes. Rabbit moved off the table and laid down on the floor. He started to hum, and Delany lazily kicked at him. He stopped.

Rue and Taver strolled through the front door together, so close they were practically touching. They were whispering but stopped as they got closer. Rue said hello, and asked if we were doing well.

"Doesn't matter," Delany said, taking her elbows off her knees and sitting up. Rue gave her a little smile.

"He dead?" Taver asked, nodding towards Rabbit. He had closed his eyes at some point.

"No," he answered, not opening them.

"Too bad," Taver said, and it sounded like he meant it.

I looked at Delany and realized she was looking past Rue and Taver. I followed her gaze back to the front door, where the most gorgeous woman I had ever seen was walking towards us. Dark brown skin, hair wrapped in a splotchy orange cloth, and a loose skirt wrapped around her. She looked more ready for a runway than a prison.

"Hey Noel," Delany said, like it was nothing.

Rabbit opened one eye. "No second?"

"No, and when I do get one, if you come near them, I'll snap every one of your dainty little fingers off," Noel said, pleasantly.

"As long as it's not my—"

"Hey Brock," Delany said, loud enough to cut Rabbit off. He mumbled something and closed his eyes again. "This it for today?"

"Yeah," Brock said, moving to stand next to me. Delany eyed the distance between the two of us.

Rabbit sat up. "Not Pitt?"

"No, he's expecting a delivery," Brock said. Rabbit perked up. "Nothing you would be interested in." Rabbit's shoulders fell.

Noel took charge. "What are we discussing today?" Slowly, everyone turned to look at Delany.

"Someone doesn't want to light people on fire anymore," Rabbit said when Delany didn't say anything. I had to admit, she was very good at looking disinterested. Even with everyone staring her down.

"I think it's unfair," Delany said. "We should give them a choice."

"No," Rue said, not offering a further argument.

Noel wiggled her head back and forth, as if mentally weight the options. "We don't have to kill them right away. They aren't much of a threat until they go crazy. That takes some time."

Rue shook their head once, firmly. "It's better to be safe than sorry."

"It's better to be compassionate than cruel," Noel said quickly.

"Killing them is compassion," Brock said. Rabbit, still on the ground, looked from person to person, like a tennis match. I realized I was probably doing the same.

"Burning is compassion?" Noel asked, cocking her head at Brock in a way that somehow managed to come across as demeaning.

"Until one of them gets out and kills us all," Brock said. "I'm not saying I enjoy it, but we have to get rid of them as soon as possible. It's a safety issue."

"As soon as possible? They sit in there for days at a time," Delany said, sitting up. "You really think letting them sit in there for days is better? Let them run into the fence. It's quicker."

"Besides," I added, "Those cages won't hold forever." Everyone was looking at me, dead silent. "If Pittman or someone his size gets in there, do you really think that metal will hold?"

Delany pointed at me, as if to agree with my point.

"We've never had anyone escape before," Taver said, though it was unclear from his tone what side he was taking.

Rabbit stood up. "You would know, you've been here the longest, old man." It wasn't meant to be a helpful statement. "And Noel," he turned to look at her. "The fuck? Compassion? We let people starve to death. Some Pink guy straight up murdered another one for a piece of scrap metal. He wanted it as a roof. We can pretend we have a system and some order here, but it's a fucking nightmare. I'd kill any one of you if it meant I could live ten minutes longer." I squinted at Rabbit. He had just told me about a justice system and all that. I wondered if he was full of shit then, or now.

Rue nodded. "We give people entertainment, something to look forward to."

Noel had locked eyes with Rabbit, completely ignoring Rue. Suddenly, she looked over at me. "He's cute, huh?"

she asked, with the hint of a smile. She had a good foot on Rabbit, towering over him. Rabbit didn't look concerned in the slightest, but she looked ready to pounce.

"Listen, it doesn't matter," Taver said. "I don't give a fuck when you kill your infected, whether you do it thirty seconds after they get bit, or ten years after. As long as they don't infect anyone else, I don't give a shit." He paused his scolding to look at everyone in turn. "Unless you are so deeply rooted in your beliefs that you think your people will fight anyone over it, shut up."

Noel gave a little smile, as if she had won something. Her smile was just as mischievous as Rabbits, but she was way more intimidating. He was a cat after a mouse; she was a lioness after a zebra.

Everyone was quiet for a little bit, the scolding sinking in. "Anything else?" he asked.

"Yeah," Delany said. "We are going to have to make new places for the new Reds to stay."

"No our problem," Rue said quickly.

"It will be when they start fighting for supplies," Delany said. "We have to make a deal."

"With who? We don't have shit," Rabbit said, leaning against the table.

"Pink has empty houses," Delany said. "Four of them." It was quiet for a second. "I want your support when we take them."

"Take?" Rue repeated. Delany blinked.

Everyone seemed to be thinking for a second. Brock sighed. "They aren't using them, then fine," he said. "Green has no problem with it." Rue gave him a look, but Brock didn't seem to care.

"Purple concedes," he said, sounding somewhat reluctant. Noel nodded. Rabbit sighed and said he didn't care.

"Anything else?" Taver asked. No one spoke up. "Good. Bye." He turned and walked away, and if I didn't know better, I would have sworn he was stomping.

As everyone started to wander off, Noel grabbed Rue by the arm. I gave Delany a look. She noticed too, but she nodded no. I followed her out of the building.

Rabbit, of course, trailed behind us. "Hey, Heather," he said, trying to keep up with us. Delany kept walking, so I did as well. "Heather," he said again, hitting his leg on something. "Fuck. Hey."

When we were outside, Delany stopped and let him catch up. "Relax, momma bear," he said to Delany's stare. "I'm harmless." Delany rolled her eyes, and walked off. I didn't follow her, and she never checked to see if I did.

Rabbit gave me a smile. "She likes me, even if she tried to kill me that one time."

"What?"

"Oh, it was a while ago. I took a few things that didn't belong to me, she was upset, I told her to fuck off, it—well, it's water under the bridge, right? Listen." Rabbit looked around. "I heard you got money."

"If you heard that, you heard wrong," I said, crossing my arms. Whatever direction this was going, I knew I wasn't going to like it.

"So you're broke?" Rabbit looked like someone had sucker punched him.

"Yeah."

"Damn." He paused, then answered my question before I had to ask. "I heard you had money. I wanted to get some stuff in."

"And you thought I would give you bribe money?" I asked, then realizing. "Oh, you don't anymore. What happened?"

"Just a temporary snag," he said, running his hand through his hair. "I got some plans." He took a step away from me, then seemed to remember something. "Don't tell anyone I'm low, alright? I owe some favors, and it won't go well for me if that gets around. I'm serious." He didn't threaten me, like Delany would have. He looked sad instead, desperate even.

"Yeah," I said, nodding a little. I wanted to ask him why he was giving drugs away the other night if he was low, but he sauntered away, disappearing into the crowd of houses.

Back in Red, people were wandering around, chatting. It was getting dark, and people usually started to disappear around now, but there was a buzz. I ran into a few Reds I knew by name and asked them what was going on.

"Yellows throwing a party," Tina said, rubbing at her elbow. "No idea why, but Rabbit's gonna be there, so it's gonna be a good time." She smiled at me, like we both knew a secret. "You should come."

I thanked her and went to find Delany. She was sitting in the house, playing some game in the dirt with her finger. "Hey," I said as walked in. "Tic-tac-toe?"

"Something like that," she said, letting out a little sigh. "What did Rabbit want?"

I hesitated. Rabbit told me not to tell anyone, but he and Delany were friends. Surely it wouldn't hurt. "Nothing," I said, sitting down across from her. "Wanted to see if I knew anyone on the outside." She raised an eyebrow. "Apparently he wants to expand his market." Delany grunted but didn't say anything.

"Want to play?" I asked. Quickly, she ran her hand over the dirt, wiping away the game.

"No."

I wanted to ask if she wanted to talk about it, but I figured she didn't. We sat quietly for a few minutes, both of us looking at anything but each other. "We keep track of who dies," Delany said quietly. She reached over and grabbed a small black book. She tossed it to me.

I cracked it open. The first page said "Red" on the top, like a title. Under it, a list of numbers and dates. The first date was about ten years ago. I flipped the page. More numbers, but not all of them had dates. As I turned a few more pages, there were no dates anymore. Every once and a while, there were names instead of numbers. Steven, Lola, Marcus.

"Why do you do this?" I asked, turning another page. The handwriting changed every few people, sometimes were written in cursive, some so poorly written I couldn't read them.

"Angel used to do it for me," she said, almost in a whisper. "I can't write."

I looked up at her. "You can't—" I remembered that she was born in the prison. "Do you want me to write in Michelle?" She nodded, softly. There was a pencil tucked into one of the pages, so small it had to scrunch my hand up weird to hold it. I flipped to the last page with writing on it.

I expected to see Angel's name there too, but it wasn't. I looked up at Delany, about to ask if she wanted me to write her in too, but she was looking at the ground. I wrote Angel's name down, then Michelle's. I tucked the pencil back into the book and handed it to her. She took it silently.

I heard her sniffle a little. "I'm gonna go," I said, standing up. I barely realized what I was doing. "Yellow's having a party." She nodded again, and I quickly ducked out of the house.

I didn't actually want to go to a party. I wasn't even sure what constituted a party here, but I was pretty sure I didn't want to be a part of it. I went into town hall instead and sat against the wall for a while. I wondered why no one else seemed upset about what happened the other night. I couldn't even think the words "burning" or "murder". No one else seemed phased, but Delany. I wanted to start asking people how long they had been here, maybe I could figure out when I would be okay with it too.

A few people walked through the town hall, and in the distance, I could hear two people's mumbled conversation. I didn't want to go look at Delany. My heart broke for her in ten different ways. I didn't have a lot of family either, and I couldn't imagine losing any of them like that.

I debated sleeping in town hall that night, but there seemed to be a general consensus against that for whatever reason. I assume it had something to do with fighting. I stood up and walked, thinking I might try to sleep at Pittman's little house, if there was room.

I had to walk by Yellow to get there, though, and the sound of so many people talking and laughing and yelling made me feel a little better. Someone was beating on something, something that sounded metal, as if it were a drum. There was another, fainter drum sound as well, but I couldn't tell what that was from. Someone else was singing off key.

As far as parties go, it seemed like one. The little walkways between houses were full of people, some of them so thick it didn't seem like there was a way through it. *Pittman is probably here*, I told myself, justifying my curiosity. I walked into the fray.

I had barely made any progress when, while turning a corner, I ran straight into Rabbit. He grabbed me, one hand on each elbow, to stop us from actually running into each other. "I—" I started to say, and he cut me off.

"Listen, there are like three hundred people here, and I see you like six times a day. If you have a crush on me, you can just say so," he said with a smile. I pulled my arms away from him.

"If you weren't always lurking around, maybe you wouldn't see me so much," I said, trying to walk around him. He stepped out in front of me.

"Nothing else to do but lurk," he said, "You gonna hang around for a while? Come on, I'll set you up." He tried to reach for my hand, and I pulled away from him. "Oh, come on. I don't have cooties and I'm willing to bet you're hungry."

"We all are, stupid," I said, but it lacked the same kind of gusto he had.

"I'll return you to your momma afterwards," he said, "promise." It was dark, almost completely pitch black now. I could hear people, but I could only vaguely see those who were directly in front of me. He took my hand and put it on his shoulder so I could keep a hand on him as we moved. He led me back to what I assume was his house.

There were maybe four people in the little house that really should have only fit maybe three. I couldn't really see them, but I could hear them. They were laughing at a joke we must have missed. They barely said anything when we came in, but I could hear them shuffle around to make more room for us.

Rabbit sat, and I did as well. I was about half way out of the doorway. I could hear something, but I wasn't sure what the noise was. It sounded almost like crunching. "Here," Rabbit said, reaching over and fishing for my hand. I gave it to him and he put something in it. Before I could even ask what it was, he told me just to take it.

I put it in my mouth and swallowed.

◆

Someone was poking me in the cheek. "Hey." It was Rabbit's voice. I opened my eyes and rolled my head to look at him. He cracked a smile. "Morning." I didn't say anything, I just squinted at him. "You gotta get up, Delany's looking for you."

"No."

Rabbit let out a loud laugh. I closed my eyes.

◆

"Rabbit, get the fuck away from me. Heather?"

It was Delany. *I should wake up.* Why wasn't I waking up?

"What did you do?"

"Nothing, she took it from me. I only asked once. I was a perfect gentleman. I didn't even leave her alone with Raymond."

"Yeah, Raymond the Rapist, how kind of you." Delany sounded angry. "If you come near her again, I'll skin you alive."

"With what? Ow, shit, okay, okay, I'm gone."

"Heather? Hey, Heather?"

◆

I opened my eyes and I was alone. I tried to say something, but my voice wouldn't work. I tried to sit up, but my arms wouldn't move. I lay there for a few minutes, looking around. I was in Delany's house, but I have no idea how I got there. I had no idea where she was. It was either sunrise or sunset, I wasn't sure yet.

I don't know how long I was awake before Delany came back inside. "Hey," she said, softly. "Are you okay?"

I tried to talk again, and coughed. "Yeah," Delany said. "You've been here for what, five days? You're already getting mixed up in this shit."

"Sorry," was all I could muster out.

"Sit up," Delany said. "I've got water."

I still felt like I couldn't move, but I tried. Slowly, I managed to get somewhat upright. Delany watched me struggle, but didn't help. "Here," she said, handing me the chipped cup. I drank everything that was in it, though it wasn't much.

"What did he give you?" Delany asked as I set the cup down.

"I don't know," I said, closing my eyes. "I don't think I asked." I could hear Delany sigh. We sat there in silence for a while

◆

"So, you're sick?" Brydie invited herself into the house and sat down on Delany's blanket. "You don't look sick." I had no idea where Delany was. I figured she asked Byrdie to watch me.

"I am," I lied.

"Am I going to get sick?"

"No."

"Good, I don't want to be put in a cage."

"I'm not that kind of sick."

Brydie shrugged. "I don't know, you look terrible." I looked at her. "It's true." We sat there for a few seconds, but it was clear Brydie was itching to ask me something. I decided to wait until she asked on her own.

"What did you do to get sent here?" she asked, looking at me. "A bunch of people don't think they did anything, so we think they're in a gang. Are you in a gang?"

"What? No, I didn't—" I stopped. "I don't remember. I don't think I did anything."

"That's what they keep saying," Byrdie said, giving me a sideways look. I rolled my eyes.

"Who is 'they'?"

"Farha, Skidmore, Torres, Palm-something, I don't know how to say it," Brydie said. "They all said they haven't done anything wrong."

"Well, we must have," I said, moving so I could lay down again. "We're here, aren't we?"

Byrdie shrugged. "I heard they are starting to send people here for no reason," she said, looking at me. I wondered if I should lay down with her here—she did kill someone after all. I figured I would be fine, there was nothing around that she could use as a weapon. "You know, to see what we would do with them."

"Who told you that?"

"Margret said that Pittman told her that," Byrdie said, nodding. "They said it's a rumor, but I think it's true." She was quiet for a minute, and I closed my eyes. "You don't seem like a bad person, like us."

I woke up again I could hear people outside. Byrdie was still sitting across from me, tracing things in the dirt. I sat up, slowly, and looked around.

"You were asleep that whole time," Byrdie complained. "I wouldn't have come here if Delany had told me you were going to sleep."

She ran her hand over her drawings to erase them. "I should go, I'm hungry." I nodded. "Are you going to be okay?"

"Yeah, I'll be fine," I said. Byrdie stood up, and I did the same. I was starving as well; my stomach felt like a pit. "I got to find Delany," I said, rubbing my head. Byrdie nodded.

"Good luck." She skipped out the door and back towards her house. I walked towards town hall.

Delany was in the middle of the building with Noel. I walked up to them, realizing I hadn't eaten in who knows how long, but I was doing okay. I wasn't dizzy or confused anymore. I felt good. Sure of myself.

"Delany," I said, getting ready to apologize. Before I could say anything, Delany, very calmly, lifted her arm, made a fist, and struck me in the face. More out of shock than anything else, I fell backward.

On my ass, I looked up at Delany. I didn't know if Noel knew what happened or not, but she looked indifferent towards Delany punching me. Delany and I held eye contact for a second before she offered me her hand, and I took it.

She lifted me back to my feet, then went on talking to Noel like nothing had happened. "So you think that's true then?" Delany asked, "nothing like that has ever happened before."

I wanted to ask what was happening, but my jaw didn't feel so great, and I figured Delany wouldn't be happy if I butted in. So I waited.

Noel shrugged. "That's what my friends tell me." Delany didn't seem to like the vagueness, but she didn't' say anything. "If it is true, then we need to prepare."

Delany nodded. "We have to assume it'll be us verse them, right?" Noel nodded. "Then we need to stick together."

Rabbit and Taver walked in together, whispering to each other as well. Delany looked at Rabbit like she was trying to skin him alive with only her eyes. "We got bigger problems, Delany," Rabbit said, joining us. "Looks like we might be getting a little bigger soon."

"Apparently the other prison has three hundred people," Taver said. "We don't have room for that."

"See, I heard we were the ones that were moving," Noel said. "They're saying 'merger', no one knows who is moving where."

"Wait, another prison is coming here?" I asked, and everyone looked at me.

"Shit happens when you aren't around, you know," Rabbit said. "We didn't all just take the day off because you did." I wanted to punch him. I could feel my heart speed up, like my body was getting ready for a fight while my head tried to talk me out of it.

"Yes," Noel said, ignoring Rabbit. "We just found out." Behind her, I could see Rue walking in.

"I think the groups need to join together," Delany said, looking around. "We don't know what these people are going to be like, or what kind of system they're going to have. And especially if we move. Who knows how things are going to change?"

"You think they have a king?" Rabbit asked, eyes wide, "Oh, if they do, then I get to be our king." Everyone looked at him. "I've been a leader the longest."

"And yet," Delany said, looking at him. He crossed his arms.

"Oh! What if we go to a prison with running water!" Rabbit practically screamed. "Dude!"

No one paid attention to Rabbit. Rue shook their head. "No, we aren't picking a king. We'll act as one, but if and only if we have to."

"What does that mean?" Taver asked.

"Or they might kill all of us. What if it's a prison just like this, but they have guns? They would just mow us down—" Rabbit was still rambling.

"We might be getting more supplies, we might not," Rue mused. "They might be better armed than us, or have something we don't. If we are in a position of weakness, we can work together to fight them. If not, I don't see any reason to change what we are doing."

Everyone sort of looked around. "Either way," Rue continued, "we can't do anything without knowing anything. We'll have to wait and see."

Delany and Rabbit both opened their mouths, but someone else started screaming.

Everyone turned to look behind me, the direction of the screaming. Vaguely, through the machinery, I could see someone flailing.

"Fuck," Delany said as she pushed past me and took off running. Rabbit and Noel followed behind her. I looked back at the others, who didn't move.

"It's safer here," Brock said with a little shrug.

"Fuck you," I said, then took off after them. I don't know if it was adrenaline, or I had somehow managed to learn how to move through the machinery in the last two minutes, but I caught up to Delany and them just as they got to the screaming.

It was Byrdie. She looked so little running in circles, throwing her arms around. There were three bats chasing her, one latched onto her arm already. She screamed wildly, throwing herself to the ground, then back up again.

We watched her for a second, then Delany went back into the building. There was a loud crash, and she came back out with a small pipe. Rabbit tried to grab her, but Delany swung at him. He barely got out of the way. Noel grabbed me and pulled me out of Delany's warpath.

Delany started to swing at the bats, hitting one of them on the first try. It screamed and tried to fly at her, but she hit it out of the air. It fell to the ground and she brought the pipe down on it hard enough for it to practically explode. The three of us took a step back.

There was a crowd gathering on the other side of the bats, but everyone was staying pretty far back. Most people were huddled up in houses, just peeking through windows and doors to see the action. No one was getting close.

Delany struck at another bat and missed, hitting Byrdie in the back. She didn't apologize, she just kept swinging. I looked over to Rabbit, who rolled his eyes a little. Noel looked pained, like it hurt her to watch. I decided Noel was my favorite of the leaders.

It took five or six swings, but Delany got the other bat and killed it too. The only one left was the one on Byrdie's arm. Byrdie herself had taken a few good hits with the pipe too.

Delany didn't seem to know what to do about that one. She tried to hit it with the pipe, but Byrdie was still screaming and flailing, and no amount of asking her to stop was going to work. I pulled away from Noel, who still had a firm grip on my arm.

"If something happens to her, we need you," Noel said over Byrdie's screams. I hadn't thought about that. With new people coming, we couldn't *not* have a leader of the Red. At the same time, I wasn't sure I wanted to be around to see what happened with the new people.

I pulled away from her again, and with a bit of a sigh, she let me go. As I walked over, I took off my shirt. "Hold her," I told Delany, who didn't move.

"Heath—"

"Fine, hit her. Just get her to stop," I said, hiding my hands in my shirt. Delany held out the pipe and tripped Byrdie.

Now on the ground, I put my foot down on her to keep her in place. "Get ready with that," I said over my shoulder to Delany. I think she realized what I was doing. At least I hoped so.

Byrdie was still flailing, but the bat was latched onto her. The bats were huge, like the size of a hawk or something. It took up more than half of her arm. It took a few tries, but I got my shirt around the bat and pulled. It was in there pretty good, and I could feel Byrdie's skin pulling as I tugged on the bat. I ripped as hard as I could, and the bat came off. Along with a chunk of Byrdie's skin.

I threw the shirt down quickly, before the bat could bite me, and Delany started to smack at it until it didn't move anymore. Byrdie was on the ground, holding her arm, crying. I almost offered her my hand.

Delany looked around. "Alright," she said, loudly. "Get the torches."

It felt like three seconds, but it had to have been longer. People, of every group, came out with sticks and torches and pipes, just like Delany had. They swarmed, focusing in on Byrdie. They poked and prodded her, waving torches at her, steering her towards the cages. We were on the dead opposite side of town so they had a while to take her.

Delany and I didn't follow the crowd. We stood there, around the dead bats. "What do we do with them?" I asked, looking at the blood spots. They were beaten and then trampled—I didn't see a good way of removing them.

Delany was quiet. Noel stepped forward. "We can use some of the little metal scraps like shovels and throw them through the fence." She sounded sure of herself, like she had done this before. Delany looked at me and nodded.

It didn't take long to scoop the bats up and toss them away from the town. We had to toss my shirt, too. "So, they're locking Byrdie up?" I asked as the fence buzzed. Delany nodded. "And then you have to kill her?" She nodded again.

We walked back to the town hall, and the group leaders were still hanging around. "That was stupid," Rue said as we got close. "Are you bit?"

Delany shook her head. "Both of us are fine," she said.

Brock nodded. "We'll talk tomorrow. If the bats are out, we should leave." Everyone seemed to agree to that, and scattered pretty quickly. Before Noel headed off, she unwrapped the cloth on her head.

It wasn't a shirt, but she wrapped it around me to make one as best she could. "This is important to me," she said, her hair twisted into knots. The wrap had given her a very regal look, and with her so close to me, she seemed friendlier now. "Don't fuck it up."

Rabbit gave us a nod as he left. "Repping Orange now?" he joked, then winked at me.

Delany and I walked home together, which wasn't far. "Thanks," she said quietly.

"Rabbit was right," I said, looking at her. "You are a sap."

Delany gave me a look like she was about to punch me again. "You are too."

"Yeah."

◆

Red didn't have the town hall anymore, so I had some time to wander. Delany didn't seem to care what anyone did, as long as we didn't get in a fight with anyone else. It made sense, it didn't seem like the time to get the groups riled up.

I walked around the Red group for a while. People who came in with me were starting to build their own places. I could see two girls carrying a large piece of metal—probably taken from Pink—down a walkway. Some boy was making what looked like a castle out of mud, and I realized it was the beginning of a wall.

I thought about making a place myself, somewhere I could hide out if I wanted to. Something told me not to, that being close to Delany right now was a better idea. Things were about to change, and we didn't know how. It didn't seem like the right time to leave.

I thought about going to the cages to see Byrdie, but I didn't want to. Seeing Mitchell took a toll on me, and I didn't even know her. I didn't know Byrdie that well either, but I had no desire to see her locked up.

I walked around town hall, then wandered through the Orange group for a while. No one seemed to care that I was there, everyone was busy talking and trading and living their lives. No one spoke to me, though. I had entered this clique, this group of "leaders", and I realized I had no other friends. Even people in Red group who would say hello to me didn't say much else. I felt incredibly lonely.

When the sun was close to setting, I ran into Rabbit outside of Pink group. I didn't even see him, he just came up and grabbed my arm. "You need better reflexes," he said. I had jumped, but I hadn't tried to get away from him. Now, I ripped my arm away.

Rabbit reached out and tugged on my make-shift shirt. "Everyone's got a soft spot for you, huh?" I pushed his hand away. "Why is that?" I realized he wasn't joking, he was looking for a serious answer.

"I don't know," I said, looking at him. I didn't know what he wanted me to say.

"What's your last name?" he asked, crossing his arms. A shiver ran up my spine.

"What does it matter?" I asked. My back was to the town hall, but I knew there was an opening in the wall close by. I didn't know why I felt the need to run, but I did. I tried to remember exactly where the opening was.

Rabbit licked his lips. "You got three of us to like you. And Freddie and Brock don't hate you either."

"You're an idiot," I said, defensively. "Maybe I'm just a nice person."

Rabbit shook his head. "No, you're not. It's something else."

I rolled my eyes. "Did you want to tell me something important, or can I leave?"

Rabbit smiled. "I have a friend who's a guard."

"That's really interesting, Rabbit." I started to walk away. He grabbed my arm, hard, and held me in place.

"He knows your last name."

I didn't move. "So?" I asked. I knew that there was nothing special about my family, no reason why I shouldn't want Rabbit to know my last name. But I didn't. It was this eerie feeling, like everyone knew something about me that I didn't. And I wasn't sure I wanted to find out.

Rabbit looked me over. "Either you are the best liar I ever met, or you're an idiot."

I played it off as best I could. "Okay, Rabbit."

Rabbit shook his head at me and let go of my arm. The second I was free, I turned and walked away from him. "Tell Aunt Felicia I said hello!" he called after me. I didn't say anything and tried not to look like I was in a hurry as I walked off.

I ran into Delany back at the house. She was sitting on the floor, looking at the little black book. It almost looked like she was reading it for a second. "Where have you been?" she asked me as she tucked it away.

"I ran into Rabbit," I said, shaking my head, as if trying to brush the experience away. "Actually," I said as I sat down across from her. "He mentioned my Aunt Felicia."

"Yeah," Delany said, like she knew what I was talking about.

"Wait, did he tell you?"

"That your Aunt was also in prison? Yeah, he mentioned it," Delany said with a little chuckle. "He was practically giddy."

"She's in prison?"

Delany looked at me for a second. "Did you not know that?" she asked. For some reason, she seemed more annoyed than confused. "Yeah, she's been in prison for a while, apparently."

"For what?" My only memories of Aunt Felicia were vague, my mom had stopped talking to her years ago, though I was never actually sure that we got the full story about why. It was just something we accepted.

"Rabbit doesn't know yet, his guard is still working it out," Delany said, cracking her fingers. Each one popped loudly, one after the other. "But he thinks it'll help him figure out what you did."

"I don't know what I did," I whined. "Why is he so irritating?"

Delany smiled. I hadn't seen her smile in a while. "He's just like that, I guess."

Part Three
CLAP

I woke up and sat straight up. For half a second, I thought it was the new people, coming to invade the prison. I had been having nightmares about it for three weeks now. It was pitch black, but I could hear the rain slapping the side of the house. It sounded like a stampede outside. *Not an invasion, then.*

CLAP

The house lit up for a second, bits of light sneaking in through the cracks in the walls. Delany's side of the house was the one getting soaked with rain.

"Delany?" I called out, over the sound of the rain. Nothing. "Delany? Delany?" Still nothing.

My mother had been terrified of storms. Every time one came through, she made me hide in the closet with her. I had hated it and tried to explain how we were safe inside, that the storm couldn't get us.

Now, it could. The house felt like it was seconds from blowing away, I could feel a raindrop or two cross the gap from Delany's side of the house to mine. I wished I had a closet.

I felt around the floor, and another flash of lightning went off. I could see for a few seconds, just enough to find my shoes. I slipped them on and stood up, my hands out in front of me. I felt the walls- which were damp already— and found the doorway.

I always hated that few seconds between the house and the car when it was raining. Now, in the dark, I would have to try to find a hole in a building filled with junk, hopefully not impale myself trying to get inside, and also find Delany. I took a deep breath. *No big deal.*

I stepped outside and felt the cold rain on me. I felt like running, but with nowhere to run and being unable to see, I had to take baby steps forward, using my feet to feel out my next step.

"Heather?"

I didn't know who was calling my name, I could barely hear it over the wind.

"Heath—Hey!"

Someone grabbed my arm, and I pulled away. "Hey, hey, it's Tiger." I could tell the person was screaming, but I could still barely hear them. "I'm Noel's friend. Come on, I'll get you inside."

I let the hand take a hold of my arm again, and I followed where it led. It didn't take long for them to find the town hall and get me inside.

"You okay?"

I still couldn't see, but I felt a sense of relief like no other. The wind wasn't as loud, the rain seemed further away, and the lighting wasn't as threatening.

"Hey, Heather?" the person squeezed my arm. Now I could tell it was a boy's voice. "You okay?"

"Yeah, sorry, I just—my mom hated storms," I said, as if that explained anything.

"It's alright. Did Delany just leave you like that? Oh, Noel is going to kick her ass. Come on," he said quickly. I could almost hear the faint smile in his voice. He took my arm again. He moved slowly, also trying to feel his way around. "They usually—ow—usually light something on fire so we can see, but I guess no one knew the storm was coming."

I could hear other people talking now. Tiger kept a hold of my arm as we got closer. "Hey man," he said, and we stopped. "Yeah, Delany just left her."

"Noel is going to kill her."

"I know, that's what I said!"

I couldn't see anyone who was talking. My eyes hurt I was opening them so wide. "Tiger," I said, barely above a whisper.

"Yeah, yeah, I got you," he said, and we started moving again. I could hear him slap hands with someone else. I had no idea how he managed to see a damn thing.

We were moving through a crowd of people now. I had no idea how he could see, how he was navigating. It seemed like he was just bumping into people and moving along. "Delany?" he called after a few feet into the crowd.

"Over there!"

"By the back!"

"Back there!"

A few people called out at once, trying to help us. Tiger called out a thanks, and we started moving again. "Delany?" he called again.

"Over here!"

Her voice was like being wrapped in a warm blanket. I pushed past Tiger—he gladly let go of me, and I fell right into Delany.

"Get off me," she said, pushing me back. I was soaking wet, but she was as well. I had no doubt she had been running around out there, helping people get into the building.

"Dude, you can't just leave her," Tiger said from behind me. I reached out and touched Delany again, her shoulder. She pushed my hand away.

"Sakar's house got hit," she said, somber. "We put it out, but—they burned."

"Oh," Tiger said. "Then yeah, I guess you can leave her."

The idea of another human, probably only a few feet from me while I slept, burning to death didn't faze me at all. "I didn't know where you were," I said to Delany. She reached out and tapped my arm, quickly.

"I'm right here. I was getting the kids inside. I knew you would be fine," she said. For a second, her voice was tender, comforting. It didn't last long. "Come on, we have to find something to burn. It's dark as dicks in here."

She took my hand and we walked through the dark together.

I woke up again, and Delany was gone. There was a mess of people around, sleeping on the floor. I had seen pictures of school gyms during hurricanes, where people were sleeping on cots, crammed in together. This was like that, but with no cots, food, or any kind of medical supplies.

I sat up and looked around. Delany, of course, was nowhere to be found. As far as I could tell, almost all three hundred plus of us were in there, sleeping almost back to back, bent and contorted around the old metal machines. Most people were still asleep, except for the few people creeping around, trying to pit pocket.

It had to have still been early; the sun was barely coming through the holes in the building. I got up as quietly as I could, tip-toeing over sleeping bodies as I made my way outside.

I came out on Green's side. The cages had withstood the night—I could hear the infected screaming. Green looked okay, all in all. Their gardens flooded, and now looked like little mud patches, but the houses were still standing, albeit, some at an angle. As I was looking around, Pittman rounded one of the corners.

"Checking out the damages?" he asked me. I nodded. "Come on, I'll walk with you." He walked over to me, getting a little too close. "Sleep okay?"

"No," I answered. "You?"

"Like a log," he said. "I heard Orange and Red got the worst of it. This shitty building kept the wind from us." Pittman slapped his hand against the bricks as we walked.

"Yeah, Delany said something about a house burning down," I said, trying to remember the name of the person she had mentioned. I had no idea.

"I heard," Pittman nodded.

We walked through Yellow. They seemed alright, one or two roofs gone, but nothing a day's work couldn't fix.

"How bad does it have to be for them to come help?" I asked. "The mythical *them*."

Pittman shrugged. "I don't know. We've had half the people here die from the fucking flu, and nothing. One time they came and gave us food for no reason. Another time, Red caught on fire and they showed up in twenty minutes. Who fucking knows?"

I wanted to say that I bet they did that on purpose so that we couldn't force them into coming to help us. I didn't get a chance to. As we rounded from Yellow to Orange, Pittman and I stopped.

It was flat. Everything that had been standing before was gone. Everything. There were piles of wood, broken and ragged, a few odd bricks, some cloth wrapped up in all of it. I could see straight to Red, where only a few houses stood.

"Fuck me," Pittman whispered. "Fuck."

"How many—" there was a lump in my throat, and I swallowed it. "How many people do you think died?"

Pittman shook his head. "Five? Thirty? Who knows? I didn't see too many Oranges last night."

A shiver ran up my back. There were a few Oranges, picking around the wreckage. "You go," Pittman ordered. "Go find Delany and help. I'll get them." He didn't wait for me to answer. He took off at a jog, helping an Orange lift up a large piece of wood that was once a wall. I could see a dark red stain on the wood.

I ran to Red. "Delany?" I yelled at the Reds who were picking through the fallen houses. We were better off than Orange, it looked like only a third of our houses were gone.

"Over there," Kayla pointed further down. I nodded and took off again.

I found Delany carrying someone by the arms, while a girl named Susanna carried their feet. I ran up to them, jumping over a pile of bricks. "Are they okay?" I asked before I could even see.

I wish I hadn't looked. A brick must have fallen on their head, right in the center of their forehead. Their head was completely smashed in. "No," Delany answered, flat. "No."

The rest of the day was a blur. Moving wood, making a pile of bricks, pulling another body out from under a house. Someone else was crying in the background of everything, though I could never seem to find them. Delany took off running, then came back twenty minutes later with blood on her knees. I cut my hand on a broken board. Someone from Purple gave me some water.

The Reds and the Oranges were staying in the town hall for the night. We didn't need a meeting to decide that. Someone from Yellow came by and told Delany that they were holding a meeting at the archway. She nodded, and he took off.

"You go," Delany said as she looked around. Her hands were on her hips, like a mom looking around at the mess her kids made. "I have stuff to do here."

"I'll help," I said, "I want to."

"No, you'll go to the meeting," Delany ordered. She took a breath in, then went back to what she had been doing. It was still cloudy, and the wind was picking up again.

I waited a few seconds, giving her a chance to change her mind. Someone started yelling, and we both looked. Three Reds were chasing four Yellows, who had bricks in their hands. Delany didn't hesitate and took off after them as well.

I watched until they disappeared into the crowd of people and houses. I took a deep breath in, looking at what was left of Red. We didn't look too bad, now that we had cleaned up all day. But it would take time to repair everything. I just didn't know what we were going to do in the meantime.

I turned and walked through what was left of Red towards the archway. I was the last one there. "Sorry, I—"

"Delany's not coming?" Noel asked, arms crossed.

"No," I said. Rabbit huffed. "But I can take care of it. What's the plan?"

"The plan for?" Rue asked, one delicate eyebrow raised.

"For rebuilding?" I answered. "Is that not what this meeting is about?"

"No," Noel snapped. "This meeting is about how big their dicks are. They don't want to rebuild shit."

"I don't have shit to rebuild," Brock said firmly. Pittman wouldn't meet my eyes.

"Fuck you," I snapped, and everyone looked at me. To be honest, it kind of shocked me too. "This isn't just our problem. Red—"

"Is overpowered, has their heads up their asses, and thinks they run shit," Freddie finished. "Orange's only useful contribution is cloth, so." She made a face at me. My arm tingled a little, as if asking me to punch her.

I looked at Rabbit. He looked back at me, blank-faced. "You're high," I said, looking at him.

"Yes ma'am," he answered, nodding his head so hard his mop of hair flew around.

"Get out of here then," I snapped. He didn't move, and I pushed him. "If you aren't going to be an active member, get lost." He stumbled, and I pushed him again. He took a few steps forward, then looked back at me. "Go." He kept walking.

I turned back to the group. "Listen, we just need—"

"No," Rue said, quickly. "This is not a negotiation. You have nothing to offer us."

I looked at Noel. Her eyes were fire, ready to burn. But she clearly didn't have a plan either. "Fine," I said, looking at each of them in turn. "But the next time you need—"

"We won't," Freddie said, cutting me off. "I'm leaving." She walked off, and the others followed her.

"Noel," I said, reaching out for her. She pulled her arm away. "We have to do something."

"What? We have nothing," Noel said, crossing her arms again. "I swear, I could beat them all to death, but—" She let her voice fade out.

"No," I shook my head. "We have to think of something."

"I lost half my people, I can't fight a war," Noel said. I would have sworn I saw her shiver. "We can't do anything."

What would Delany do, I thought, taking in a breath. "Oh, shit," I said, reaching out for Noel again. She took a step backward. "We don't have to do anything!"

"What?"

"No, Noel, listen. What have we been fighting about this whole time? The infected. We don't want to burn them anyway, right? So let's not."

"But if the cages—"

"Exactly," I cut her off. "We just wait them out. They'll get worried the cages won't hold, and they'll cave. Blue and Green are right next to the cages, they'll cave first. Pink isn't big enough to fight us on it, Rue will do whatever Brock says, and Rabbit is always high."

Noel blinked. "What if they just burn our people?"

"It'll take them time to get to that point. Delany has refused before, and they waited her out. She did it. This time, she won't."

Noel thought for a second. "That actually might work."

"So listen," I was speaking faster and faster now, excited about my plan. "We rebuild, we help each other. Red wasn't hurt too badly, we'll send people over to help you. In the meantime, we wait for them to cave."

"And if we finish rebuilding by the time they cave?" Noel asked.

I shrugged. "Then they owe us."

Noel nodded. "Are you sure Delany is fine with this kind of alliance?"

I didn't hesitate. "Yes."

◆

"You came up with that?" Delany asked me. She was sitting on the ground, a half-eaten strawberry in her hand.

"Yes," I said, almost breathless. I gave her the entire transcript of the meeting. She just nodded along the whole time, eating strawberries.

She nodded again. "Alright. What do you know about building houses?"

I shrugged. "I took a technology class where we build bridges once. But I do have some ideas for the houses."

"Good enough," Delany said, and she ate the rest of the strawberry, leaves and all, and offered me her hand. Sticky and wet, I took it and pulled her to her feet.

She wiped her hands on her jeans. "Alright," she said, nodding. "I want you to take ten Reds and go help Orange."

"I wanted to—"

She held up her hand. "Go help Orange."

"No," I said, standing my ground. Delany looked at me like she might hit me. "Let me tell you how to make the houses more stable first, then I'll go." Delany didn't say anything.

"Look, we were just putting them on top of the ground, and pushing dirt up along the sides of the walls to keep them up, right? If you dig a trench and put the walls in it, it will be more stable. Like, I don't know, five or six inches down?"

"That'll make the house five or six inches shorter," Delany said, crossing her arms.

I shrugged. "House won't fall down, though." She grunted at me. I took that as a dismissal and headed over to Orange.

Two weeks after the storm, and no one even whispered of a merger. It was a burning day, and nothing else mattered. Everyone gathered by the cages. They were full this time, all fourteen of them. The screaming was almost unbearable. Rue started the ceremony, as per usual. I could barely hear them over the yelling, from the infected and the crowd.

I watched as Rue burned their people, then Brock, then Freddie. Rue called up Delany. I couldn't hear, but their eyes shot straight for us. Delany, Noel, and I had gone to our spot in the back, leaning against town hall. Delany made eye contact with Rue and smiled. She did not move.

"Delany," I couldn't hear Rue, but I could see their mouth forming words. "You have to."

Delany did not move.

Rue waited a full minute, while the crowd roared. I could hear some people shouting that she was a bitch, or a witch, that we should burn her instead. She didn't move.

Rue called Noel. She didn't move either.

This one really got the crowd going. Noel had never refused before. Rue looked like they had been slapped, then their look softened. I think they realized what we were doing.

"What if they burn them?" I asked Delany, no longer confident in my plan.

"Then they burn them," she answered.

Rue set the torch down and told everyone to go home. No one moved. They got louder, angrier. It was hard to tell, but two people up front started fighting. It looked like an Orange and a Blue.

"Where are the Reds?" Noel asked, watching the Orange grab the Blue by the hair and throw them.

"Here and there," Delany answered. I looked around and didn't see any either.

"And they know?" Noel said. Delany nodded.

◆

The cages were full again. This was the furthest along I had seen any of the infected. One girl, a Red, who was already far along last week, hung from her cage bars upside down, banging her head against the metal.

"Looks like it might break," Noel said, leaning herself against the town hall.

"That's why we're all the way back here," Delany said.

Rue went through the motions. Bizarre how burning people seemed routine to me now, like it was just what we did on Sundays. I watched Delany. She still flinched every time, just like the first time I had been there. I wanted to be like that, to grow up with all of this, and still flinch.

The Red cages, four of them now, shook. Not a single one of them were people anymore, they were completely gone. Two Orange cages were filled as well, a boy who screamed the entire time, but barely a yellow patch on him, and a girl so wild I knew she would break out first.

Rue spoke, and they burned. Brock burned. Freddie burned. Rue called Delany. She cocked her head to the side, twirled her hair between her fingers, and smiled. Rue didn't wait long this time. They called Noel. She spit on the ground.

Someone came up, a Pink, to yell at Delany. She pushed herself off the wall and stood toe to toe with him. He was maybe a full foot taller than her, towering over her little body. I couldn't hear what she said to him, but slowly, trying to save face, he backed up.

Rue started to talk. They were saying something—it was hard to hear—about the importance of unity and protecting each other from the infected.

"They're going to burn them," Noel said.

"Yeah," I said. "If they don't grab him first." There was something cold in my voice, something I didn't recognize. I liked Rue. I mean, I didn't *dislike* them. I knew at the end of the day, they were trying to protect their people. But I was trying to protect mine, too.

The wild girl, the Orange one, was upside down now too. Rue walked up to her first, torch outstretched. I couldn't see what happened, she must have grabbed the torch and pulled it towards her, because Rue was jerked forward. And then they screamed.

Everyone was screaming, and running away. We waited. Rue's body stumbled backward, a deep red flowing out of their neck. Delany let out a chuckle.

"Fucker," Noel said, a smirk on her face. "We should have done this a long time ago."

Rue's body fell to the ground as people ran away screaming. We watched, silently. Until the cage started to shake. Delany pushed off the wall. "Come on," she said, grabbing my hand. Noel followed behind us.

I didn't look back, but I could hear the cage hit the cement as it fell.

I had seen stampedes in documentaries, were thousands of zebra all ran at once, for no reason. Or wildebeests ran across a river full of crocodiles. Or people ran into a store on Black Friday. I had never been a part of a stampede.

As far as running went, I was okay. I did track in middle school, I knew how to breathe. Delany was next to me, holding my hand, pulling me along. I heard more metal— I wasn't sure if it was a cage or a house falling down. But I could hear the infected Orange girl screaming. In my mind's eye, she was launching herself at us, jumping twenty feet in the air to land on us. In reality, I didn't look back.

We ran. Noel was next to me one minute, then gone the next. I tried to say something to Delany, but she just tugged on my hand even harder. We ran past Red, straight under the archway and into the field. Now, everyone was spreading out.

"What's the plan?" I huffed at her.

"Fence," she said. "Get our backs to it, get the infected to run into it."

I had no idea how Delany had come up with a plan that quickly. All of my mental energy was going towards not tripping and not peeing myself. We were getting closer and closer to the fence. There was a loud noise, almost like a plane, but softer. I figured the houses behind us were falling like dominoes. *So much for rebuilding*, I thought.

We were about ten feet from the fence and Delany stopped. She turned around to look at me, letting go of my hand. She looked ready. I wasn't sure for what, but she was ready.

"Heather!" she screamed, and I heard a crack. Within seconds, my vision went black, and suddenly, I could feel cool, wet grass against my cheek.

Blind, I heard another crack, a softer one, and felt a puff of air. *Delany fell too.*

Made in the USA
Columbia, SC
26 August 2022